Guarding Heaven

A novel by

Joe DiMarino

PublishAmerica
Baltimore

First printing

ISBN: 978-1-4489-6171-9
PUBLISHED BY PUBLISHAMERICA, LLLP
www.publishamerica.com
Baltimore

Printed in the United States of America

Guarding Heaven

Chapter 1

Detective Daniel Lambert of the Frederick Maryland Police Department was not very happy. Instead of heading home to celebrate his daughter Carrie's fifth birthday, he was crouched down in a Weiss Grocery Store in response to a 211, possible armed robbery. He was looking for employees, customers, good guys, bad guys. He would be happy to find somebody but he wasn't finding anybody, and that was very disturbing to him. The store seemed completely empty. That alone was enough to raise his suspicion. No store should be completely empty during business hours.

"This is Detective Lambert on scene at the Route 40 Weiss Grocery Store in response to the 211," he whispered into his two-way radio. "I can't find a soul in the goddamn store. This might be a fucked up situation."

"Language Daniel," scolded a voice in the radio. "This is an official frequency."

Recognizing the voice of dispatcher, Julie Turkelton, Lambert replied, "Hi Julie, I know that, but I'm not supposed to be on official business. I was just walking into the store when the 211 went out. Deb wanted me to pick some things up on the way to Carrie's party."

"Oh yea, that's right, "Julie responded. "Tell her happy birthday for me."

"Thanks, I will," Daniel said. "First I have to find out what's going on here then I have to get some dog food."

He realized that his ex-wife would be furious if he showed up at his daughter's birthday party without it. Though he couldn't for the life of him figure out what dog food had to do with a five-year-old's birthday party.

"That's bad timing Daniel. Maybe you should sit tight until back-up arrives. Two patrol cars are on route and should be there in just a few minutes."

"Thanks for the advice, Julie, but I think I'll look around a bit. Stay tuned."

"Just be careful, Daniel, you don't want to ruin Carrie's party."

He heard the concern in Julie's voice as he put the radio in his pocket with his left hand; at the same time he pulled his Glock 23 revolver from its holster with his right.

Crouching he went from end cap to end cap. He silently scanned down the length of each aisle as he passed. He chuckled when he came to the pet section. Maybe he could pick up the dog food his ex wanted while he was here. At that very same instant, Lambert's muscles tensed in response to a shadow that came into sight at the other end of the aisle. Realizing they afforded little if any protection at all, Lambert knelt behind some bags of dog food anyway. *At least he was somewhat hidden from view,* Lambert thought as he aimed his gun and calmly but loudly said, "This is Detective Daniel Lambert of the Frederick Police. Please come out so I can see you. But take it slowly, very slowly."

"Fuck you shit head," came the unexpected response.

Daniel immediately fell to the floor in the firing position. At the same time, a man jumped into the aisle with his gun aimed directly at the spot Daniel had just been.

Restraining his trigger finger, Lambert shouted: "Drop your…"

But he stopped when he saw the flashes coming from the gun. "Definitely a bad guy," Lambert said aloud to himself. He didn't need his fifteen years of police experience to figure that out. Lambert ducked, and then fired twice. He watched as the man fell, clutching his throat.

"Shots fired Julie," Lambert spoke into his radio as he slowly made his way to the man he had just shot. "You better send an ambulance."

"Roger, Daniel, I'll call for an ambulance. Your back up is on scene."

Not really hearing what was coming out of his radio, Lambert looked down at the man he had just shot. The giant pool of blood and holes in the man's throat and forehead left him now with no doubt that he was dead. Lambert was an expert shot but in his decade and a half on the force he had never shot anyone dead before. He was still trying to take it in when he heard a woman's voice scream, "Help us" from the next aisle.

Instantly back on alert, Lambert peeked around the corner and saw a woman and child. The woman was cowering on the floor in obvious abject terror. Standing next to her was a young girl, probably her daughter. She seemed to be the stronger of the two—or maybe she was too young to realize what was going on. She was gently stroking her mother's hair in an attempt to console her. Not seeing anyone else, Lambert made his way to them. "I'm a police officer. You're safe now. Are you hurt?"

In the next instant Lambert felt a stinging pain in his shoulder. Lambert knew he had been shot and he also felt himself falling as his feet came out from under him. But before falling completely he twisted his right arm behind his back and got off three shots straight behind him. The fall didn't hurt as he came to rest with his left arm trapped under his waist and his right arm twisted oddly next to him. *Damn it*, he thought as he saw that his gun had landed way out of reach. He looked at the young woman. She was uttering "OH MY GOD, OH MY GOD" over and over again like some religious mantra. The child was now clutching her mother's arm. She was not making a sound; she just stared at Daniel, unblinking and not moving.

"Shut the fuck up, bitch," a voice said from almost directly above him. I guess it was too much to hope that his backward shots would have hit this scumbag. "You and your brat are next, but first things first. Say your prayers, pig."

Lambert could sense the man directly over him. He could visualize him aiming his gun. He could feel the man's surprise and hesitation as Lambert rolled over to his right drawing his Smith & Wesson back-up gun from its belt holster with his left hand. Ignoring the incredible pain in his shoulder, Lambert raised his gun and fired. The look of surprise in the assailant's face was quite satisfying to Lambert as he saw the hole instantly appear directly between the man's eyes as his shot found its mark. He watched the man fall backward dead on his feet. The soft nose bullet literally blew the back of the man's head off—taking half the man's brain with it as it exited.

Daniel knew he was hurt but he felt he would live, especially with help so near at hand. He knew he wouldn't be able to get up but he turned his head towards the woman and girl to make sure they were okay. *I guess I'll be ruining the party after all*, he thought. He then said to the woman,

"Everything will be fine; more help will be here soon…"

Daniel stopped short when he looked past the woman and saw the little girl holding the gun he had dropped and pointing it directly at his head. *No way*, Daniel thought. *This kid thinks I'm a bad guy*. Daniel guessed the girl was about five—Carrie's age.

Would she know how to use that gun? Of course she knows how. Any kid who ever played a fucking video game or watched any television would know how to pull a trigger. He knew he would have to convince her that he was a good guy. As he began to speak Daniel saw the girl's trigger finger tightened.

"No Sara, no," the mother shouted.

But it was too late. The chamber had already ignited and the bullet was exiting the muzzle. In less than a hundredth of a second the bullet traveled the three feet to Daniel's head. Before that second had past the bullet entered Daniel's frontal lobe, shattering his skull and pulverizing his brain. And as the bullet retreated out of the back of his head, Daniel Lambert, Frederick Police Detective was dead.

Chapter 2

Daniel remembered being shot and he knew that he should have died. Modern medicine was capable of miraculous things but that little girl shot him at point blank range. He looked up into the distance and said aloud, "Holy Shit, there really are pearly gates." He was staring in amazement at an incredibly large, incredibly golden and incredibly shiny set of open gates. The gates were attached to marble columns at least as tall as a five-story building. It seemed incongruous to Lambert that the gates and columns stood there unattached to anything else. They just stood there, all by themselves, surrounded by a white landscape. As Daniel surveyed the scene he almost expected to see puffy clouds filled with angels. But there were no clouds or ground or anything else he could describe—it was just white and featureless. *I am either dead or having some kind of fucked up coma-induced dream*, he thought as he continued to take in the surrounding environment. Everything seemed so bright so he figured that he must be dead and he was seeing "the light" that many near-death survivors reported seeing. *I guess I should go into the light*, he hesitatingly decided. Though the scene from the movie Poltergeist where the miniature medium kept telling the girl to go into the light and the girl's father kept telling her not to go in to the light came to mind. Of course for Daniel, wherever he looked everything looked the same, incredibly bright and incredibly white.

Daniel, not being sure of his current situation, closed his eyes and took a deep breath. He felt his chest heave but he wasn't sure what he was breathing; the *air* had no smell or defining characteristics. He looked down and saw that he was completely naked. Clothes apparently didn't convey into the afterlife—if that was where he was. He did wonder what clothes his mother (or his ex-wife) chose for him to be buried in. He hoped they chose casual clothes—he really hated wearing suits. *What an odd train of thought, I don't even know if I'm dead, or dreaming or where the hell I am and I'm worrying about my funeral clothes. I am one fucked up dude. No wonder Deb left me.*

As his train of thought returned to the present situation, Daniel realized he felt a little uncomfortable standing in an unknown place—confused, naked and alone. Out of habit, Daniel looked at his left wrist to check the time. Of course his watch was not present but he was surprised and pleased, to see his anchor tattoo on his bicep—something familiar in a very unfamiliar place.

Looking around Daniel realized that he had not moved since arriving or materializing or appearing or however he got to wherever he was. Not having any idea as to where he should go he decided to head towards the most obvious, and for that matter, only landmark visible—the gates. As he began to walk Daniel thought how nice it would be to have something on his feet, his Sperry Topsider boat shoes would be perfect. As quickly as this thought came into his mind, his familiar, well worn, topsiders appeared on his feet.

Hmm...I think about my shoes and like magic, they appear. Daniel smiled with this discovery. Having at least some kind of control over events made him feel a little more comfortable. Deb had always said he was a control freak. She called it his cop mode whenever he took charge, and it drove her nuts.

Armed with this newfound power, Daniel decided to dress himself. The ambient temperature wasn't cold, or warm for that matter, so a pair of shorts and polo shirt would be perfect. Instantly he was attired in his favorite khaki shorts and blue Izod shirt.

Feeling a little better he restarted his trek towards the gates. He became conscious of solid ground underfoot as he walked. It wasn't grass or dirt or cement or wood or anything familiar, but it was solid and he wasn't falling through.

Getting closer to his destination he began to appreciate the real size of the gates. His first estimate of five stories seemed to be about ten times too low. He also began observing figures milling about the gates. Not a few, not even a few hundred. It seemed to Daniel to be thousands, if not tens of thousands of people milling about though generally heading towards the gate. Though the throng was too large to really pick out individuals, he could discern that the incredibly large crowd was also incredibly diverse. He saw whites, blacks, Asians, Indians, man and women. It was basically a cross sampling of the total human population—though he could not see any young children, which registered as a little odd but he gave it no further thought.

Daniel had never seen such a mass of humanity. Many were completely naked, though most had figured out what he had and were wearing clothes of an very large variety including western garb, oriental robes, Arab coverings, etc.

"Mr. Lambert, Mr. Lambert, over here," A man's voice just appeared in his head. It didn't seem to be coming from anywhere in particular; rather it seemed to be coming from everywhere. And in the next instant Daniel found himself in a white room across a desk from a middle-aged man who beamed with an ear-to-ear grin.

"Greetings Mr. Lambert, and welcome to the next phase of your existence. My name is Philip McKenzie. I am a Greeter and I am here to introduce you to Heaven."

What the fuck? Daniel thought as he felt his brain constricting and contorting and basically melting down. Everything, the whiteness, the gate, the throngs of people, Philip McKenzie, were becoming too much for him to handle. He just stared at the man sitting across from him not saying a word. He just stared.

"I know it's hard to grasp," said McKenzie. "But trust me when I say you will be just fine. You are not the first and God knows you won't be the last. As a matter of fact you are the 121 billion, 246 million, 342 thousandth 177th human to enter Heaven. We currently admit roughly 150,000 arrivals in a time span equivalent to one Earth day."

There was true compassion and genuine niceness in McKenzie countenance and tone, and Daniel, who had always considered himself a good judge of people, liked him immediately. And from the gleam in his eyes to the smile on his face, McKenzie looked to be trustworthy and genuine. As the realizing that McKenzie was okay solidified in his mind, Daniel began to calm down.

Daniel took a deep breath, "I feel better now. I'm still not sure if this is real or some kind of crazy dream, but if it's real I guess I'm relieved to be here instead of the other place... Is there another place?"

"Oh yes. There is another place and it's horrible, truly dreadful. It's worse than you can even imagine. It's so bad it's called Hell," he said with sardonic grin. "But forget all about that nasty place for now." He swished his hand in the air as if whisking away all thoughts of that place. "Let's talk about Heaven, which you will find is completely different that any image of heaven that mankind ever came up with."

"I don't know about that. The whole Pearly Gate thing seems pretty clichéd." Daniel looked around the desk for something—a pen, a paper clip, anything—to fiddle with. Of course the desk was completely empty so Daniel just folded his hands together and laid them on the desk.

"Oh, so you saw Pearly Gates," McKenzie replied, ignoring Daniel's fidgeting. "Some people see statues of Buddha, some see a bright light, and some see rainbows. It really doesn't matter. The image is only there to allow new arrivals to get their bearings, so to speak. It's like a celestial lighthouse that helps calm the fears of the newly departed, which in this case are the newly arrived." McKenzie laughed again. To Daniel he seemed like the type of man who loved to laugh and tried to find humor in any situation. McKenzie settled down and asked, "It helped you, didn't it?"

"I guess it did. So who or what are you? Some sort of Angel, I'm guessing."

McKenzie laughed again. "Don't be silly, there are no angels in Heaven, just people, normal everyday people—who just happen to be dead. Of course our very being—our existence if you will—is very different than it was on Earth." McKenzie leaned forward as if he was about to impart some great words of wisdom or an important secret. "Now, though I'm not an angel I was a teacher in my previous existence, which is almost the same thing as being an angel. When I was alive I always loved teaching and helping people so when I died and was reborn, as we say in Heaven, I became an official greeter. A *Heavenly Welcome Wagon*, if you will." He reached out and grabbed Daniel's hands and shook them warmly as if greeting a long last friend. "So welcome to Heaven!"

"Wait a minute Mr. McKenzie," Daniel freed his hand and sat back out of McKenzie's reach. I realize you are here to help me but it seems that every sentence you utter just confuses me more. Maybe you should start explaining before my head fucking explodes." Daniel felt bad about the swearing but just like when he was alive it was a habit he couldn't break.

"Of course Daniel, I can call you Daniel, can't I? And please call me Mac." Without waiting for a reply he continued. "Now, first thing—just stop worrying. You are in Heaven for pity's sake, Heaven! You made it, you should be so proud. But not too proud, that's a no, no as you'll find out," Mac chuckled as if he had made an inside joke. "Also I should tell you that everyone that dies comes here." Mac noticed Daniel's confusion so he said reassuringly, "It's not important that you know everything immediately, no cramming here. You have all of eternity to learn, after-all."

"So let's begin with the basics," Mac continued without taking a breath. "And the basics are this; God exists, Heaven exists, Hell exists, and the Devil exists. God created everything. He, and I only use *he* just for simplicity, is not really a he or she. I'm also not to sure about the created in *his own image* concept. So God is not a he or she. He is nothing and everything. He exists everywhere and nowhere. Frankly we learn much more about who or what God is in Heaven than we knew on Earth and that's still not that much."

"I never believed in a God as some beneficent ruler sitting on a cloud and I guess I was right about that,' Daniel said. "But boy was I wrong about everything else.

Mac smiled and then continued. "He created Hell in order to contrast Heaven and he created the Devil to contrast his goodness. You can't have up unless you have a down, after-all. He then created the universe. He created it with a bang a very big bang, if you will. God is very hands off in Heaven as he is on Earth. The universe evolved very nicely and pretty much as humans have figured out through the ages."

"Life eventually appeared on Earth and just as Darwin said, all living things evolved through natural selection. That is until about 150,000 years before you were born Daniel. Do you know what happened then?" Mac asked and waited for a reply.

"Well I think that's when humans first appeared," Daniel answered as if responding to a teacher—which was in reality what he was doing.

"That's very good Daniel. You are now my prize pupil," Mac said as if he knew what Daniel was thinking.

"I wonder if he can read my fucking mind." Daniel thought.

"No, I don't know what you're thinking, but after doing this job for 20 years I am pretty attuned to my charges' thoughts," Mac said.

"To continue…there is no real time in Heaven as we knew it on Earth. Time only has relevance as you interact within your current reality. For example, we have been conversing for about five minutes, but the passage of that time has no relationship to any other existence within Heaven. This is a tough concept and you will learn more about it as you go."

'Now where was I? Oh yea, Homo sapiens—oh how I love that term—came on the scene winning out over other human ancestors such as Neathradal. Now Homo sapiens had evolved the same as all other species. God took an interest and He decided to endow all humans with something special. That something is our divine *Essence.* Our soul, if you will. He gave us free will and an opportunity to have eternal existence in heaven. Now free will is quite simply the ability to do good or evil and to know the difference. As you live your life on earth you do good things or you do evil things and your soul reflects the personality you develop as you make choices throughout your life."

"Because God gave humans free will he also left an opening for the Devil who had not been doing much since his creation except biding his time. He was starting to think that he might be spending his eternity alone in Hell with the various ghouls had goblins he had conjured up. Now the Devil is one evil genius. As soon as he could he imbued in humans the desire for seven traits which may sound familiar: vanity, jealousy, gluttony, lust, wrath, greed and, sloth."

"The seven deadly sins," Daniel said eagerly.

"Exactly Daniel," Mac said with real enthusiasm. "Were you a religious man?"

"No, not at all," Daniel said a little too embarrassed to mention that he knew of them from a movie. "Why did God let him interfere with his creation?

"I'm not sure if he just wasn't interested in the actual *goings on* back on Earth. Or maybe it was what he had planned to happen," Mac answered. "Now the seven deadly sins are just the labels we put on those traits. I forget who it was that first named them, it was some monk, but they are really instinctual. They are not really sins or anything they are just vices that can make a virtuous person viscous. They are bad habits and should be avoided. And they aren't exactly as they were named."

"So gluttony doesn't mean overeating on Thanksgiving," Daniel said pleased but not surprised that Mac laughed.

"And sleeping in on a Sunday does not mean you are slothful," Mac added. "Of course just because humans have the desire to commit these vices it doesn't mean they must act on them. In our souls are some pretty powerful virtues to compete with the Devil-given indulgences. They are: prudence, temperance, courage, justice, charity, diligence and faith. Your last act on earth, saving that young mother and her child might not have shown much prudence but it did show diligence, after all it was your job. It also showed your sense of justice. You knew the bad guys were committing an injustice. Of course you showed plenty of courage, you really were brave, Daniel. But most important of all you showed charity. You were willing to give up your life so they could live."

As Mac spoke, Daniel to his surprise felt no incredulity at all to what he was hearing. He understood and comprehended all that Mac was speaking "The Truth" as only an emissary of Heaven could speak "The Truth." All of the human arguments he remembered from his life just didn't matter any more.

The proselytizing from the religious crowd just didn't matter any more. The pontificating from know-it-all academics didn't matter any more. The religious fervor of the zealots of the *Non-Religion*, Atheism, didn't matter any more. The indecisiveness of the 'I need proof' agnostic just didn't matter any more.

At this very instant, all that mattered for deceased Detective Lambert was that he was dead, but not just dead, he was, as unbelievable as it was to him to think about, in Heaven.

"So, what do you think so far?" Mac said after taking a deep breath. "I find this whole heaven thing fascinating. When I learned the basics, and that's what I'm teaching you now, just the basics, I found it to be easily understood. So much of what you need to get along here is intuitive"

Daniel shook his head. "I'll take your word for it Mac, I have no choice, but right now I'm still pretty unsure of how I should live in Heaven."

"My suggestion is to live just like you lived on Earth."

"I wasn't what you would call saintly when I was alive," Daniel said.

"You knew then and you know now what is good and what is bad. It's called instinctive knowledge, or intuition," Mac said as he made air quotes. "It is one of human kind's links to God and also a gift from God. Throughout history most of our knowledge of there being *more to it than just this* was instinctive and not based on rational process," Mac explained as he began teaching again.

"Knowledge of God is apriori knowledge, meaning you know it's true without actually observing it. Posteriori or empirical knowledge is gained from actual observation. I know there is a good looking man by the pool because I see a good looking man by the pool. Well the good looking part may be opinion," Mac chuckled.

"I didn't realize that I had to learn Latin in Heaven. Because except for hapeus corpus, I sure didn't use it much in life," Daniel said sarcastically.

"Sorry about that chief," Mac apologized. "I was a philosophy instructor at The University of Chicago when alive. I guess that's why I ended up doing this job after I died."

"How did you die?" Daniel asked. Not really sure if that was proper, he added, "If you want to tell me."

You can ask me whatever you want, silly boy." Mac responded. He then told Daniel that he had died in 1987 from complications due to AIDS. "What was that tasteless joke back then?" Mac continued, "*What's the hardest part about getting AIDS? Convincing your parents you were a hemophiliac.* The irony is that I, a homosexual man, contracted AIDS from a blood transfusion."

"I was very happy to learn, when I arrived in Heaven, that AIDS was not a plague sent by God to punish us wicked deviants. The same goes for the bubonic plague, polio, cancer and every other disease that affected us as human beings. These things were and are just part of the evolutionary mish mash that is life on Earth."

"Now enough about me let's get back to religion. The basic tenet of most religions is to treat others as you want to be treated. Of course, just as there are bad people there are bad religions," Mac said. "Satan or devil worship is bad, evil if you will. So are religions that abuse or mistreat humans or animals. In my opinion, for what it's worth, the worst religion or pseudo-religion is self worship. Worshiping ones self is a disgrace in the eyes of God. It goes against all of the heavenly virtues and plays into the vices."

"It did seem as if people were becoming more and more selfish during my lifetime. There was a lot of 'what's in it for me' and 'win at all costs' attitudes permeating society," Daniel interjected

"That's what you would expect, considering that the Devil holds sway on Earth. Now as I said God did give mankind hints of Heaven. He also sent some messengers. And some of the messengers sent by God ended up being the catalysts for the formation of the great religions. Moses, Jesus, Buddha, were all directly influenced by God. Others, such as Mary Baker Eddie, Confucius, Gandhi, Joseph Smith, Martin Luther and Martin Luther King and a myriad of others that no one has ever heard of, were influenced by their on awareness of God." He scrunched his face as he said; "Now they all didn't get it exactly right, and some were pretty wacky, but most of what they preached was good." Mac sat back and folded his hands behind his head and looked seriously at Daniel.

"Of course throughout history some very, very bad things were done in the name of religion or God. Off the top of my head there were the inquisition, terrorism, witch hunts, to name a few. But they were really done by either badly mistaken men or by men following there own agenda."

"To contrast the bad things there were golden moment on Earth when good triumphed or at least held evil at bay. Catholic Monks preserving all of human knowledge through the dark ages, The Renaissance, World War II and countless smaller events that are not recorded in history."

"That's why all people are allowed into Heaven. Heaven is where anyone can become as God intended, no matter how they trained their souls on Earth. We call your arrival in Heaven rebirth and all of the *Reborn* start with a clean slate in the eyes of God. Unfortunately it is very hard for a person with a corrupted soul to change and many, if not most, simply don't."

"So after making it to Heaven they don't change their wicked ways and then what? They go to hell, don't they?" Daniel asked.

"That they do," answered Mac. "And some go pretty quickly. Hitler didn't last too long before he was rounded up and sent bye-bye. He was the source of many *problemos*, trust me. He had hooked up with some of his cronies and sycophants. He was trying to establish the Fourth Reich here in heaven. He truly belongs in Hell and that's where he will spend eternity. May he rest in *un-peace*."

"What about the criminally insane?" Daniel asked. "I know many were faking but some really had a screw loose and couldn't comprehend good from evil."

"They come to Heaven with their screws tightened and have an opportunity to a happy existence," Mac said, obviously very happy with that fact.

"You mentioned some people revert back to the bad behavior they lived on Earth. Who rounds up these bad guys?" Lambert was getting real interested. Forget all that religious stuff—Good guys and bad guys was something that he understood. "Is there some kind of Police Force of Angels?"

"Not Angels, just regular guys and girls and they are called Guardians," replied Mac. "Guardians are reborn police officers, constables, detectives, and other law enforcement types from all over the Earth and from all over time. You have New York City Coppers and Sengali tribesmen and Roman Legionnaires and British Bobbies—well you get my meaning. Though most have some sort of Law Enforcement experience from their life's, the one common denominator of all of the men and women who serve as Guardians is that they had impeccable moral character, soul character as we say here on the other side."

A thought came to Mac's mind as he recalled that Daniel had been a police officer during his life and he asked, "Would you be interested in joining?" Mac couldn't hide the hopeful anticipation in his voice as he waited for Daniel to answer.

"Impeccable moral character is something I might have fallen short of attaining during my life. You can ask my ex-wife, I'm sure she'd confirm this fact." Daniel felt he might be unqualified to be a Guardian and he was a little disappointed.

"Pish posh," Mac said swishing his hand again. "You are a fine man who would make a fine Guardian."

"Well if the powers that be think I have what it takes then there is nothing I would like better." Daniel responded without hesitation.

"Well that's just super. Even though you still have a lot to learn, I am finished with your introduction. Remember that Heaven's reality is your reality. You can go where you please by just thinking of that place. You'll get the hang of it, trust me." Mac suddenly looked very serious and he looked directly into Lambert's eyes, "And please Daniel, never forget that there are only seven real rules to follow in heaven." As he spoke he extended a different finger from his closed fists ad he counted. "One, don't be too vain about yourself; two, don't be jealous of others; three don't be gluttonous or overindulgent in you're the things you do; four don't lust inordinately after anything; five keep your anger in check, anger leads to many bad actions; six don't be greedy and seven don't be lazy." He put his hands down and continued, "Two more important thing Daniel; Do unto other as you would have them do unto you, and all things in moderation and moderation in all things"

With that Mac was gone and newly reborn Daniel Lambert stood alone in a now all too familiar white environment.

Chapter 3

Daniel found himself in what he figured was Heaven's version of an office. It was very well lit, though there was no obvious source of the lighting. It was similar to the place where he spoke to Mac. The biggest difference was the line of desks along the wall. Standing next to one of the desks facing Daniel was an honest to goodness 19th century British Bobby. The uniform looked meticulous. Every gold button secured, a silver whistle attached to his belt. On the desk next to him was the familiar black helmet with the distinctive silver badge that Daniel had seen in so many movies.

"It' not a very pretty place, is it?" the man asked.

"I guess it could use a plant or maybe a picture on the wall," Daniel responded.

The man chuckled and said "Aye, that would be an improvement." He approached Daniel. "William Gale formerly of Scotland Yard at your service," the man said with a slight bow. He was short, about 5 and ½ feet, but he definitely had the look of someone who could hold his own in a tussle. His sideburns and mustache were exactly as Daniel would expect—thick but assiduously manicured. His English accent was strong though

Daniel understood him easily. *What was it Mac had said; Language is not a barrier in Heaven and everyone understands everyone else. Even when they are speaking the same language,* Daniel thought.

"Hello Officer Gale," responded Daniel, "you seem to have been waiting for me, hell you probably brought me here, so you must already know who I am, correct?"

"Excellent deductive reasoning Mr. Lambert, worthy of the best Scotland Yard Detective," Gale said sarcastically but with a wink and slight bow. "But I didn't bring you here; no person has the power to transport another by thought alone. Though as Guardians we can escort a person to where we want." Gale shook his head as if he realized he was getting ahead of himself. "You will learn all of that and much more and I am looking forward to instructing you. So, are you ready to begin?"

Daniel's emotions and confusion about his whole situation suddenly encompassed him and all he could do was stare at Gale. *What the hell are you talking about? And begin what?* Daniel thought. He saw Gale look at him with concern then heard him ask, "Are you all right Mr. Lambert? You look distressed."

Daniel thought, *Distressed, are you fucking kidding? I want to pull my hair out.* But he said, "You know it's funny Mr. Gale, I have no idea how long I've been here or how long I've been dead. It's pretty fucking confusing, so, I really don't know if I'm all right or ready"

"Ah, that word," Gale shook his head slightly. "I have found that many of the more recent arrivals in Heaven use it in almost every sentence. Fuck this and fuck that, fuck you and fuck me."

"I'm sorry, I say it a lot. It really bothered my ex-wife, but it's just so engrained."

"Oh don't worry I'm not offended. I was a police officer on the streets of London after-all. We had basically the same curse words as you. Of course it was unacceptable to use those words in polite company."

"That may be true for the time in which you lived, Mr. Gale. In the time I lived the so call bad words were used in polite as well as not so polite company." He was going to add, *even television*, but decided not to considering that Gale had died long before TV was even invented.

As the conversation about the use of curse words continued, Daniel's thoughts again drifted away on a tangent. His current situation was this; here he was, Daniel Lambert, a dead cop in Heaven. He was now a Guardian—whatever that was—and he was staring at a British Bobby who was apparently his new partner. This train of thought caused Daniel considerable consternation to say the least. He did have enough equanimity remaining to make a mental note to try to control his propensity to use the F-word in every sentence. What he really had to do was get his mind straight and focus on what was happening.

"Danny Boy," Gale said using this moniker for the first but far from last time. "I know it all seems disconcerting. It's much like a newborn baby first coming into the world. For their whole existence they were warm and comfortable floating around in their mother's womb. And then, not by their choice mind you, they are evicted from their home into the cold, cruel world. We call what they go through birth and now what you are going through is rebirth."

"If you are amenable I think we should jump right in, learn by doing is always best," Gale said, then adding, "as long as no one gets hurt."

Daniel looked up at this but Gale continued, "Our first assignment is very straightforward. So if you are ready, there is no time like the present as we said on Earth."

"I am as ready as I'll ever be, Mr. Gale."

"Excellent then, Daniel, and please call me Bill or William.

Now our first assignment is Joost Visser, a young man who seems to have a problem with drugs."

"That sounds like what I dealt with everyday during my life," Daniel said. "Are there drug laws in heaven? Because if there are I hope they work better than they did on Earth."

"No not laws as we knew of them on Earth, just rules against excess and young Mr. Visser is so caught up in drugs that he needs some guidance." Gale continued, "As Guardians we have a very unique power. We can transport ourselves to another's reality as needed."

"Say what?"

"Let me explain. Each resident in Heaven controls his own reality. The only time one person can interact with another is when they exist together in the same reality. As an example, let us say you want to attend the Queen's Jubilee of 1839. That would be a normal desire for someone who was alive at that time. My wife and I were there and it was spectacular. Now if no one else wanted to attend the Jubilee you would be the only one there. Though in actuality chances are that if you went right this instant you would be surrounded by thousands of other people."

"So you are saying that in Heaven we can visit any time or place that existed on Earth? That's pretty sweet if you ask me."

"Yes it is pretty sweet as you say but you will find that most people stick with the places and times of which they are familiar," Gale said.

"That makes sense," Daniel said. "People feel comfortable with things they are used to."

Gale got back to his original point, "Now as Guardians we can actually track people down. In other words we can enter another person's reality whenever we are assigned to or if a pressing need arises. We just will ourselves there and there we are."

"That will make our police work a hell of a lot easier than it was," Daniel was genuinely pleased with this news even though he had yet to go on a single assignment in Heaven and in reality had now idea what they entailed.

"I am glad you are pleased, though I can't take any credit."

"Above you pay grade?" Daniel realized his joke didn't land when Gale ignored it.

"But since you seem ready I suggest that we now pay our Mr. Visser a visit." Gale began putting his uniform cap on.

As he was watched Gale adjust his chinstrap, Daniel wanted to say that he wasn't ready at all, but before he could speak the surrounding area begin to shimmer and change.

Chapter 4

The white office disappeared and was replaced by an expansive field of what looked like mostly mud. Rain was pouring down and Daniel felt his clothes becoming soaked. He looked at Gale and saw that he was now wearing a black trench coat. *I wish I had my slicker*, Daniel thought. And with that he was wearing his green foul weather jacket that he had worn so many times on his sailboat.

"So this is the famous Woodstock," Gale said as he looked around. "Though I was long dead when it happened I have met a few people in Heaven who were in attendance. It seems kind of dreary, don't you think?"

Daniel agreed that it was dreary, but he was also very excited. Since arriving in Heaven he had only experienced Heavenscapes. This was the first time he was in an Earth based reality and it was astonishing. He was standing in a time and place that had existed on Earth when he had been just a small child. He knew about Woodstock—he had seen the movies and documentaries about it—and he actually liked some of the music. He listened to it from time to time on the radio, though it was mostly played on the oldies stations. Unlike the music festivals of his time—which were mainly big corporate or public relations driven events trying to solve the cause de jour—Woodstock had been a down and dirty (very dirty from what he saw around him) weekend of music, sex, and drugs. In the distance he could see tall metal towers and the stage. There was a pretty large crowd of people—though not as big as he would have expected—around the stage, some were milling about but most were standing and facing the stage. He could also hear music coming from the giant speakers adjacent to the stage and on the towers. He was by no means a music connoisseur but Daniel was pretty sure he recognized a guitar riff of Jimi Hendrix. "Is this the real Woodstock?"

"Of course it's not the real Woodstock but it is Woodstock for the people here," Gale responded. "Each and every person here created this exact reality for himself or herself. We are all now experiencing this reality as if it was actually happening."

"I guess Woodstock wasn't as great as it was made out to be. Tens of thousands attended the real one. I'd be surprised if there were even a hundred here right now."

"Don't forget, Daniel," Gale said with a knowing smile, "most of the people that attended the real Woodstock are still alive. I have a feeling that after a couple more decades pass on Earth this place may be as full as the original." Daniel followed Gale as he walked toward the stage. As they got closer, Daniel saw that most of the people seemed to be getting into the music. Some were swaying back and forth others were just staring, obviously totally absorbed in the whole scene. But towards the outskirts of that central group he also noticed that there was a lot of other activity going on. And from the looks of it, it was the kind of activity that one wouldn't normally associate with Heaven. The unmistakable reek of marijuana permeated the air in spite of the downpour. People in all types of dress and stages of undress were *fooling around* in groups of twos, threes and more.

"I see plenty of non-Heavenly activity going on," Daniel said to Gale. "How do we know where to start?"

Gale stopped and turned to Daniel. "First of all, and of most importance, our responsibility is to stick to our assignment," Gale instructed. "You will soon start getting the assignments directly in your thoughts. They are just there and you know what to do. Secondly," Gale said as he started walking again, "these people may not be doing anything really wrong. You see, Danny Boy that is not for us to decide."

SPLASH! Daniel could taste the mud as he fell face first into a puddle. Spitting and sputtering, Daniel got up and wiped as much muck off his face as he could. He turned to see what or whom he had tripped over.

"Watch it man, that's just not cool," said a man whose beard and long hair were completely saturated with muddy water.

"I'm so sorry, I didn't see you." Daniel stopped talking when he saw a completely naked young lady rise out the mud next to the hippie. *A dirty Venus rising* came to Daniel's mind.

Daniel turned back to the man who was now smiling. "Free love man, the way it should have been when we lived, man. Who'd of thought dieing would really have been the stone groove they said it was. Whatever man, it was the best thing that happened to me. Peace." Then without pausing he flashed the two Guardians the peace sign then turned his attention back to the young lady and began kissing her. They both slumped down becoming encased in their mud love shack.

"Holy shit, that was weird," Daniel exclaimed to no one in particular. Then he noticed Gale laughing heartily.

"You said it Danny boy, that's some Holy Shit." The words seemed incongruous coming from Gale.

"I thought you British kept your emotions in check, stiff upper lip and such," Daniel said stifling his own laugh. "Besides, isn't that a sin?"

"I don't think it is. The closest would be Lust, but Lust is the inordinate craving for the desires of the flesh. Out in the open like that may have been unconventional in my time, but it's not necessarily overindulgence."

"Just young love," Daniel replied.

As the two officers, one from the 19th century, the other from the 21st century approached the crowd of people reliving an event from the 1960's it was becoming very apparent to one of them that Heaven was going to be very different than anything he could have imagined.

Looking at the faces of the individuals in the crowd Daniel, to his great surprise, realized that he knew exactly who he was looking for. He knew exactly what he looked like, just as if he had been studying his picture all day. He had dirty blond, long hair with a scraggy mustache. Sallow complexion with gaunt features. "Hey, William," he said enthusiastically, "you were right, I know exactly what this Visser looks like. Is that what you meant when you said the assignment would just come into my head?"

Gale smile at his new partner, "As I said that's the way it is with all of our assignments, Daniel, everything is just in our heads, as we need it of course."

No paperwork or note taking, just observation and follow-up. That sounds great," Daniel responded.

"If you should spot him all you have to do is grab hold of him and he will become locked into our reality. In other words he will be trapped and unable to flee," Gale instructed.

Daniel was becoming fascinated with this whole *reality* thing. He noticed individuals flickering in and out of this reality. It seemed to Daniel that Heaven was somewhat analogous to Internet chat rooms. You could pop in whenever you wanted, interact if you so desired and pop out at will. Of course Heaven had an infinite number of chat rooms/realities, and when you went into one your body and soul went in. You are physically present and can interact with others as well as with the environment. His muddy face was proof of that.

"There he is," he heard Gale say. Daniel looked to where Bill was pointing and sure enough, there was Joost Visser, exactly as he had pictured him. He let Gale approach him first, having no clue as to the protocol of Heavenly arrest procedure. "Hello Mr. Visser," he heard Gale say.

"Oh shit," Visser replied when he saw the two men approaching. "You just can't leave me alone, can you?" It was obvious to Daniel that the man was high on something. He could barely stand and was frenetic in his movements. He saw with surprise Visser's clenched right fist coming right towards his face. His training from life seemed to still be in place because he reacted without thinking. Right arm up to protect the face, duck towards the right, left arm straight up to deflect the punch, hard right jab into the stomach, left upper cut into the face—if needed. It wasn't going to be needed, Daniel realized, as he watched Visser double over from his body blow. "Are you all right?" Gale asked Daniel as he grabbed Visser's arms and pinned them behind him.

"I'm fine but I didn't expect that," Daniel responded.

"I'm sorry; I know I told you but I should have stressed that physical interaction with others is possible. It's also potentially dangerous and you will also feel the results of that interaction exactly as you would have felt them on Earth." Gale added, "So it might be dangerous but it also has its benefits. Just ask my wife." Gale seemed a little embarrassed so he added, "You can get hurt." Visser was a one punch man and he had given up his struggles. Gale had let go of him and he was now lying peacefully on his back on the muddy ground. He didn't look hurt and he didn't look like he wanted to escape either. "I don't think Mr. Visser has any intention of going anywhere," Gale said in another instructional moment. "But if you have hold of someone who is likely to try to escape, don't let go, they will just disappear."

"Man, you mean I can escape if I want?" Visser asked from his haze.

"No you can't," Gale snapped.

"Bummer," Visser replied and then he seemed to nod off.

"So what's next?" Daniel asked, "Do we read him his rights and take him in?"

"Of course Miranda Rights, are an American thing that some modern officers I have met were not too fond of. Here in Heaven it's not about upholding laws, there are no barristers or courts. We don't have to prove guilt. We just follow up as our assignment dictates. Sometimes we try to reason with the perpetrators and just issue warnings. But in this case Mr. Visser has gone beyond a simple warning and we have to take him to Central Booking for further action."

Daniel realized that he *knew* that, just as he had known all about Visser. Though he had no idea what Central Booking was, and he was just about to ask Gale when he saw him bend down and touch Visser on the shoulder. In the next instant the reality they were in began to shimmer and fade away. As quickly as Woodstock faded away it was replaced by another bright white room. Though this one was different than the others he had seen. Saying it was large was an incredible understatement. The room was cavernous and seemed to go on forever in every direction. It also hummed with activity. People of every stripe were milling about. Men, women, old, young. The clothes were even more astonishing. Daniel recognized dress from every culture and historical time he could think of—and an equal number that he didn't recognize.

"Greeting Mr. Gale, I see you are training a new Guardian," said an Asian man bowing slightly. The man was dressed in blue silk pajamas or at least they looked like pajamas to Daniel. "Good day to you Mr. Lee," responded Gale with a slight bow of his own. Looking at Lambert he continued. "Daniel Lambert may I present Lee Yak-yong, formerly of Chooson. He is our contact here at Central Holding. He prefers to be addressed as Mr. Lee." Then turning to Lee he said. "Mr. Lee may I present Daniel Lambert formerly of the United States. Please call him Daniel."

Not waiting for the men to act on his introductions Gale continued, "Daniel, we bring our violators here if something more than a warning is needed. Mr. Lee is a Deporter." As he was speaking, Daniel saw that Gale had transferred control of Vissor to Mr. Lee. "Central is only for habitual offenders. It's not like jail from our lives. There is no punishment as on Earth. A violator is warned, counseled and if incorrigible he is deported." Daniel noticed sadness in Gale's tone as he spoke. "In my time on Earth we used to send our deportees to Australia and the French sent theirs to French Guiana. Those were not very pleasant places and most of the poor buggers who were sent there felt as if they had been sent to Hell. Few ever returned. Our deportees from Heaven are sent away forever and their destination is the real Hell and none ever return."

"Is Visser being deported?" Daniel asked with considerable concern. He might have been a habitual offender, but it seemed cruel and unusual to send someone to Hell for *Gluttony*. It would be like condemning a shop lifter to the death penalty. "It seems kind of extreme if he is." As they spoke, Daniel watched Visser being led away by Lee. He followed them with his eyes until the two men were enveloped by the crowd.

"Not this time Daniel. But if he continues he will be." Gale did not seem angry but his tenor was stern as if he was lecturing an obstinate child. "This is not Earth. Not even close. There are just those basic rules of civility that must be followed. No exceptions."

The appealing smile reappeared on Gale's face. "Danny-boy, I know this all seems strange. I have been here the equivalent of 150 Earth years and I still don't understand how this place works. It will help you though if you at least try to comprehend that Heaven is a new life for you and it is completely different than your life on Earth. This is the place where God judges one's worthiness for eternal existence with him. Everyone comes here with the same chances. Unfortunately for many their souls are so corrupted from their life on Earth that they can not change here in Heaven. But also understand that many people are good or become good after death and do well in Heaven—they actually love it here. There are no bills to pay. There are no horrible diseases or natural disasters. You simply don't have to worry about the minutia of Earthly existence. Trust me you don't have to understand how it works to make the most of it." Gale appeared to be finished and as if on cue, Daniel saw Lee and Visser re-emerge from the crowd. Though Mr. Lee's countenance had not changed, Daniel could honestly say that he had never seen anyone look as terrified as Visser did at that moment. "What the hell happened to him?" Daniel asked Gale. "And why didn't we go? I would have liked to see the inner workings of this place."

"For his final chance at reclamation, Mr. Visser was just given a glimpse of Hell. I think it may be enough to save him. As far as going, we do usually accompany the Deporter, but I didn't want to put too much on you this soon." He then turned to Visser. "Hello Mr. Visser. I hope this experience will encourage you to change your ways."

"I…I…I…could never imagine a place like that existed." He

stammered. "And I really don't want to spend an eternity or another second there."

Daniel really wanted to ask him what he saw but Gale had taken hold of Visser and was asking him where he wanted to go.

"My grandparents on my father's side have both passed away before me. They were wonderful people. My visits to their lake house are some of the best memories I have." The terror faded from Visser's eyes as a new memory occupied his thoughts. "Do you think you could take me there?" Daniel and Visser both looked at Gale with hopeful expectation.

"As a matter of fact, we can," Gale responded. He thanked Mr. Lee and said to Daniel, "Let's go."

With that, the now familiar shimmering began and Central Holding was replaced by a new and incredibly beautiful reality. They were standing in front of a well-built and seemingly ageless log home. To the left of the house was a lake of shimmering blue that seemed to stretch for miles. The end of the lake melted in to a majestic mountain range. While caught up in the beauty Daniel was startled when the door opened. Standing in the doorway were an elderly man and woman. Both were fit and attractive people in their sixties or early seventies. Daniel wondered if one could choose his physical age in Heave or they stayed the age at which they died. That was something he would have to ask Gale when he had the chance, but for now he turned his attention to the reunion that was occurring in front of him.

"Joost, oh Joost, it is so good to see you." The woman's eyes sparkled like the sunlight off the lake behind her.

"Oma, Opa!" Visser screamed as he ran into the open, and obviously loving, arms of his grandparents.

"Our work is finished here," Gale said, as the scene shimmered and began to disappear. Daniel felt a real sense of joy in what he hoped was going to be a happy ending.

Chapter 5

The two men had no time to rest before they were *sent* on their next case. This time Daniel received the information on the assignment at the same time as Gale so he knew where they were going and who they were after. This case was similar to the first in that their assignment was not a dangerous man, just an over-indulger, though for this case it was alcohol rather than drugs. They were heading to the Caribbean island of Barbados during a Carnival celebration. Daniel guessed it was a relatively modern time period—at least the 20th century—gauging from the dress of those people not in costume. The streets of the islands capital of Bridgetown were crowded with revelers so Daniel figured that the time was early in the century—the 20's or 30's—because unlike Woodstock it had to be old enough for this many people to have died. Daniel thought about what he had been told about Heaven time; namely that it has no relevance except within a specific reality. So it didn't really matter what the epoch was only what they had to do.

The sultry evening felt good to Daniel. The tropical heat tempered by the cooling Trade winds was refreshing. The Jumby masks of the Crop Over partiers, the calypso beat of the steel drums and the smell of barbecue and spices enveloped his consciousness, and for the first time since dieing, Daniel felt very much alive. Gale led Daniel into a small bar. Though crowded, the atmosphere seemed almost peaceful compared to the boisterousness they had just left.

"Hello gentlemen," the large black man behind the bar said as they walked up. "What can I get you on this fine fete." The lilting West Indian English was pleasant and welcoming.

"If you could point out Ian Hamilton, we would be extremely grateful," Gale responded.

"Ian is right over there bothering them nice people," the bartender said pointing to a table in the corner of the bar. Sitting at the table was a young couple who were trying to ignore an obviously drunk man standing over them.

"Why don't you take care of this one, Danny Boy," Gale said to Daniel. "I'm going to pull up a barstool and ask this fine barkeep for a pint of Guinness. Well go ahead, you can do it."

As he walked over to the table Daniel realized that everything he needed to know about Hamilton was in his mind. He had been dead since 1940. Too much drink and too little health care had led to his demise at the age of 50. He had done well in Heaven. Drinking only in moderation and basically just hanging around his island home. Recently he had been visiting this Carnival reality and the party atmosphere had reactivated his urge to drink to excess. Another gluttony case, which Daniel was beginning to think, might be a common thing here in heaven.

"Hello Mr. Hamilton," Daniel said as he grabbed the man's shoulder—just as he had seen Gale do with Visser. Now that Hamilton was unable to skip out Daniel continued. "I need to speak with you."

"Of course, mon,' came the response. As Hamilton turned to face Daniel the smell of his breath-tobacco mixed with rum-nearly overpowered him. The sweat glistened on the black man's face and his eyes had the hazed over look of a man who had way too much too drink. "Ian Hamilton of St James Parrish at your service." He almost hit Daniel in the nose with his head as he bowed with drunken grace.

"Mr. Hamilton, my name is Daniel Lambert and I am a Guardian." Daniel instinctively reached for his badge. Realizing that he didn't have one he continued, "And I need a minute of your time."

As he led the man to an empty table he saw that Gale was deep in conversion with the bartender and about half way to the bottom of his glass of beer.

"Mr. Hamilton," Daniel began as soon as they were seated. "I am very new to this Heaven thing. I don't think I've been dead for a very long time and this is only my second case as a Guardian."

"And you doin a good job, if I may say so," Hamilton slurred.

"Thank you. Now you seem like a fine man and I believe you've been successful in your attempts to follow the laws of Heaven. Until now that is. What happened?"

"When I died I was sure I was for de Devil. I thought I had led a pretty wicked life. Liming all day. Drinking and making time wit all dem beautiful women, not dat dey made time back." He laughed good-naturedly. "Well mon, when I got sick I prayed so hard dat de good Lord would forgive me dat my brain hurt." He rubbed his head as if he could still feel the pain. "When I saw dem gates I was so happy I fell to my knees. After learning about Heaven I say to myself, *Ian Hamilton, your wicked ways are over. You are now goin to be a righteous man.* And I was. I live in de house I was a boy in. I fished everyday. I talked to my family, my old mates and new friends as dey passed through my life. I traveled to places I only dream of as a youngster. I went to London and New York.

I visited parts of Africa. Dem were good days, Mr. Lambert. It was glorious and I didn't miss de drink one bit."

"So what happened, Mr. Hamilton? Why would you risk all that for alcohol?"

"Well, as dey say curiosity killed dat cat. So I came to Crop Over to see why I like de Rum so much. And Lord knows I be havin a grand time. And now you is here and I may be in some trouble. Is dat right?" He looked at Daniel and Daniel saw he was sober enough to understand what he was about to say.

"Mr. Hamilton, as I said I am new to this. From what I've learned, it's pretty easy to stay out of trouble here. You don't have to worry about possessions. You don't even have to worry about necessities. But you do have those very basic and easy to follow rules. Though I have not been here long I don't think they are too hard to follow. Do you?"

"No I don't tink they be hard to follow," Hamilton answered.

"And I think I should point out that not following the rules doesn't lead to a little time in jail, as it did on Earth." Daniel said in as serious a tone as possible, "The punishment can be hell the real Hell. I just saw the look of a young man who only glimpsed Hell. If you saw the terror in his eyes, I promise you, you would never take another drink again." He tried to stay as serious as he could be, but in the back of his mind lurked some thoughts that were on the verge of upsetting his calm countenance. *I am dead. I am in Heaven. I am a Guardian in Heaven. I am on a Caribbean island during some kind of festival. I'm talking to a man who has been dead for decades.* He shook his head and continued. "I hope my visit somehow convinces you to go back to the way you were. I'm not going to do anything else and you are free to go. But please trust me when I say that following the rules is the best choice." He hoped Hamilton perceived his sincerity.

A broad grin crossed Hamilton's face. "No problem mon. I

was tinking about headin back. Dem fish may take over if I stay away too long."

With that Ian Hamilton just disappeared. Daniel looked out the window and could see the revelry was continuing. He also noticed, as he had at Woodstock, that people were popping in and out of this reality all over the place. Heaven was definitely going to take some getting used to, he concluded.

"How did everything turn out?" Gale asked as Daniel approached the bar. His glass was now empty and he signaled for two more to the bartender. "I guess it went okay. I just spoke to him and he seemed to understand the gravity of the situation." Daniel took a sip of the brown lager and couldn't help the *ah* that came out of his mouth after the beer went in. "That tastes really good," he said to no one in particular.

"Yes, Danny boy, Guinness is as good in death as it was in life." Gale said as he took a sip. "It might even be better considering it doesn't cost a farthing." He continued in a more serious vane. "Hamilton should be just fine. I see it often where people revert to their old ways, but once they realize what the stakes are many get back on the straight and narrow. Of course some don't, and I've seen some horrific deeds even here in Heaven."

"It's seems a little unfair to be drinking after we just finished lecturing someone for the same thing," Daniel said as he took another sip. He then said before Gale could respond, "Moderation is the key."

"That it is,' said the Louie the bartender who introduced himself to Daniel. "I come to this time and place because I liked it so much when I was living."

"This isn't really a job as it was on Earth? Or is it?" Daniel asked.

No mon, this is what I choose to do and where I choose to be,"

Louie said cheerfully. "I here sometimes and sometimes I'm someplace else. Whatever strikes me that's where I am."

"And when," Gale added.

"Yes and when. Though I have less control over when as I do with where. You find that so Mr. Gale the Guardian?"

"Yes I do, except when I'm on assignment," Gale responded. "It seems the when part is not fully controlled by us."

Daniel was soaking up all the information and he hoped to be able to chat with Louie the bartender for a little longer. But he knew that wasn't going to happen when the new assignment came to him. Maybe he could come back sometime; after all he did have all of eternity. He figured that a bartender would be able to give him some good insight—he assumed people would open up to bartenders here as they did on Earth. But now he and Gale had a job to do just as he finished his beer the surroundings began to shimmer, signaling an imminent departure.

Chapter 6

It was chilly in their new destination so Daniel conjured up long pants and a jacket, though Gale stayed true in his uniform. From the lack of leaves on the trees it was evidently fall or winter. The low-lying hills and rustic farmhouses hinted at a bucolic milieu. It was very similar to where he had lived in Frederick Maryland. That illusion however was shattered when he saw the sign that said Dachau. "This is a Nazi concentration camp," Daniel said with surprise and disgust.

"That it is, Danny Boy. That it is," Gale said with a shake of his head.

Though neither man had been alive when the camp had operated on Earth—Gale had already been dead for nearly a century and Lambert would not be born for twenty years—they both knew of the horrors that occurred in this place when it was running. "Many of the victims of this place come here hoping to find relatives. The nice thing is that many have. I met a man who was murdered in this camp. He kept coming back over and over. That is until the timing was just right and he meets up with his wife who had survived the camp, lived her normal lifespan, died and immediately came here also. It's was quite touching." Gale suddenly became very deliberate and serious. "But we are not here for anything like that." Daniel's eyes widened with expectation as Gale continued. "We are here to pick up a Mr. August Fleischer. He was a kapo, a um guard who was also a prisoner. Fleischer was a murderer who found himself right at home working for the Nazis. On Earth he was a sadistic evil man. When the camp was freed he fled like a coward. He was and probably is sly and cunning. He slipped away to the country of Panama without anyone taking notice. While there he carried on his blood thirsty ways, murder, rape…" Gale spat as if to show his contempt. "He died at the ripe old age of 100. Can you believe it, a man like that lived that long. When he arrived in Heaven he quickly figured out how things worked and he decided to come here to pick up where he was most happy and do what he loved, namely tormenting people weaker than him."

Daniel, of course, knew all of this. The fact that they were definitely not after a hundred year old man had answered Daniel's question about what age one was in Heaven. The answer, whatever age he wanted. Despite knowing all of the specifics Daniel felt Gale wanted to talk it out so he had not interrupted.

"I guess this will entail more than a stern warning," he said when Gale had finished. In his mind's eye Daniel could see that Fleisher no longer looked liked his age. He was big, brutish, and intimidating. Daniel could imagine the fear the prisoners must of felt when they arrived at this strange place—already dazed and confused—only to be greeted by this hulk of a man. Being a prisoner himself he would be wearing prison garb but he would have a green triangle on his chest signifying his special status. The bat he wielded in his muscular arms would confirm that status and provide a strong clue as to who he was.

On the iron gates at the camps entrance Daniel could see the words "ARBEIT MACHT FREI." Work Means Freedom. That phrase must have been cruel mockery to the countless thousands who were forced to march in and out of the gates to daily slave labor—with only death offering any hope of freedom.

In the camp people wandered about as if on a Sunday stroll. The atmosphere was far from maudlin. The cool crisp air, the colorful outfits, the smiling faces, the friendly greetings, all reminded Daniel of a family reunion and definitely belied the Earthly history of this place. People nodded to Daniel and Gale as they walked. It amused and touched Daniel to see Gale tip his police hat as acknowledgement of their greeting. How many times he must have done the same thing as he walked his beat in London so many years ago.

"It's a little different than it must have been in it's hey day." Daniel said to Gale as they walked. "I guess most of these people's deaths are infinitely better than their lives. It's pretty peaceful here so how are we going to find Fleischer?"

"He won't be strutting like the cock of the walk, not in this reality. He'll be creeping and skulking like a rat waiting for someone vulnerable. By the way, Danny Boy, this might a good time to remind you that this and all Heaven realities are real." Gale looked at Daniel. "You can be hurt and you can hurt others and you can die, or at least Heaven's version of dying. If you are badly hurt you must immediately, and I stress immediately, think yourself somewhere else."

"Did you say die?" Daniel exclaimed loud enough for those nearby to look at him inquisitively.

Daniel knew that further explanation would not be forthcoming when he saw a commotion in an alley they were passing. He and Gale both looked down the alley at the same time. "There is definitely something going on down there," Daniel said as he turned and started down the narrow pathway.

"Be careful, Danny Boy, no heroics needed here," Gale

cautioned. "Just grab Fleischer and think him to Central, no more, no less. You understand?"

"I got it. No fuc…," He was about no say No fucking kidding but caught himself before finishing, "No heroics, right. At least not until I know what kind of health care plan we got." Daniel chuckled and Gale looked at him quizzically. "Just kidding Billy Boy, just kidding," Daniel chided.

As they approached the end of the alley Daniel saw a group of six or seven people milling about. He saw one disappear, he was sure it wasn't Fleischer. The remaining people were standing in a cluster looking down at the ground. "Excuse us, we're Guardians," Gale said as they worked there way into the group. Looking down they saw two people prostrate on the ground. One was a young woman. She was holding her shoulder, obviously in pain, but she didn't look to be in mortal danger. That was not true for the older man next to her. Blood was pouring from his head and he was not moving at all. Kneeling next him was a gray haired woman. She held his head gently and kept one hand over the wound trying, unsuccessfully, to stop the blood flow. "Don't you die here Hiram, don't you dare die here. Not in this place. Not again." Daniel could see tears and love in her eyes as she spoke.

"I had some paramedic training," Daniel said to Gale as he knelt down next to the man. "Ma'am, my name is Daniel Lambert, maybe you could let me take a look," Daniel tried to speak in as calm a voice as possible. He gently pulled her hand away from the wound and held back his gasp. Daniel knew immediately that the wound was mortal. *Well at least on Earth*, he thought. Looking at the older woman he saw that she was wearing a scarf. "Ma'am may I use your scarf?" he asked gently and with a smile. She untied it and handed it to him. As he took it from her he asked if she knew the man. "He is my husband, we both died in this place in 1943." As she spoke Daniel used the scarf to put pressure on the wound. "We come here often, hoping to see a relative or friend." Daniel used his jacket to tie around the man's head and hold the scarf in place. "We've met so many, and have had so much joy and happiness, and today we find our Sharon, our beautiful grand-daughter," she said as she looked at the girl that was holding her shoulder. Daniel saw that she was still in obvious pain but sitting up and alert.

"I have checked the immediate area, the person that did this is no longer here," Gale said as he knelt down next to Daniel. "How is he doing?"

"Not good, William," Daniel said as quietly as possible. "He is going to die any minute. We have to do something and we have to do it now."

"I'm taking him to Central," Gale said as he put his hand on the man's arm. "I've never done it before but we can take anyone to Central for any reason. Once I get him there he'll be back to normal, it will seem to be about an hour in this reality. You explain to them what I'm doing." With that Gale and his charge disappeared.

Daniel looked up and saw the older woman gasp. "Its fine ma'am, my partner is going to make sure your husband recovers." He gently grasped her hand with his non-bloody left hand. "They'll be back here before you know it. How's Sharon?"

"I'm fine sir, and thank you." Sharon answered. Taking a better look at the woman Daniel could see that she was a dark haired beauty. She was dressed in 1960's clothing—matching knitted hat and sweater, white bell bottom pants, flip hairstyle—and looked to be in her mid thirties. "Will my grandfather be all right?" As she spoke she was also helping her grandmother to her feet, Daniel jumped up to assist them.

"I'm sure he is already recovered." Daniel tried to be as

reassuring as possible. "My partner will bring him back here as soon as he can. We should sit tight until they return. Do you want me to look at your shoulder?"

"No I am fine. I have been in heaven for a while now and have never had the pleasure of meeting a Guardian. Of course the timing couldn't have been better. I would never have thought of taking my grandfather to another reality." Sharon shook her had with disappointment.

"I wouldn't be so sure of that," Daniel said reassuringly.

Sharon smiled and continued. "That animal came from nowhere, swinging his bat, shouting, *Judan Swine.* How could someone be so angry after dying? He must have just seethed with rage and hatred his whole life." She didn't say this with hatred or anger it was, surprisingly, more like compassion.

"We were sent here to bring him in," Daniel said to both women. "Trust me when I say he was and is a nasty piece of work." Daniel looked around and was surprised to see that the alley had emptied out and he was alone with the two women. It felt ominous to Daniel and he increased his alertness. The older woman said to Daniel, "My name is a Sarah Jaffee, but we don't know your name Mr. Guardian."

"My name is Daniel Lambert, and please call me Daniel."

"Well Daniel," the grandmother said. "You have been so helpful. You must have been some man when you were alive."

"I don't know about that Mrs. Jaffee. I was just doing my job. You see I was a police officer in the United States when alive and that's basically what I am now."

How did you die Daniel?" Sharon asked.

Daniel gave a brief explanation of his professional life, ending with him telling of his last moments on Earth. He was surprised to see tears in both women's eyes. He was glad he didn't mention that it was the young girl who had shot him—he told them that the bad guy's shot had mortally wounded him—that might have been too depressing.

"That mother and daughter were very lucky that you were in that store, I am sure they will never forget you," said Mrs. Jaffee. "You already know how Hiram and I died. It was a dark, dark time. God blessed us though. Sharon, who was only five in 1940, escaped to Canada with her Aunt and Uncle just days before we were forced out of our home." Daniel sensed that Mrs. Jaffee was glossing over some of the details.

"I knew I would see her again and now I have," she clutched her grand-daughter's hands in her own hand. "Oh my God!" she screamed as her joy turned to terror. Daniel turned quickly and saw the largest man he had ever seen charging him with a club held high and ready to strike. "You will now die Jew lover." Daniel assumed Fleischer was speaking German but of course he heard it in English. Before he could tell the women to get the hell out of here, Fleischer was upon him. He easily sidestepped Fleischer's first swing. The big man's momentum carried him forward and Daniel launched a side kick right into the man's ribs. As Fleischer tried to turn, Daniel spun and hit him behind his right knee with a round house kick. The ex-Kapo grunted as he fell forward. Daniel knew he had hurt the giant but it would take more than a couple of kicks to subdue him. With surprising agility the giant jumped to his feet and, as he turned to face Daniel, he also swung his club. It was a clumsy swing but he still managed to nail Daniel in the left shoulder. The pain was intense, this was one strong Nazi, and Daniel felt really bad for Sharon if her blow was even half as bad as this one. As Fleischer rose his arm preparing to deliver the coup-de-gras Daniel knew he had made the mistake that all people not trained in martial arts make, telegraphing your blow and leaving your body wide open.

Being well trained in Tae Kwon Do, Daniel didn't make that

mistake. In a matter of seconds, before Fleischer club even started its downswing, Daniel delivered two open palmed jabs, one to the man's nose (Daniel felt the nose shatter from the impact) and one to the man's chin. Even though he had to hit upwards to reach the giant's face, there was enough strength in the chin blow to knock Fleischer's head back violently. As he fell backwards Daniel saw the man's eyes roll into his head. He hit the ground hard and didn't move.

"Are you hurt, Daniel?" Sharon asked anxiously.

"I'm fine Sharon," Daniel replied. "But you must be one tough young lady if that brute hit you like he hit me and you can still move your arm."

"What happened here?" It was the familiar voice of William Gale. Daniel saw that his partner and Hiram Jaffee had materialized. Jaffee looked fully recovered and his wife ran into his arms as soon as she saw him. "Our friend came back, and he was angry," Daniel said pointing to Fleischer on the ground. "He decided to take a rest until you got back." Daniel smiled as did Sharon as they looked down at the unconscious thug. "You did well, Danny Boy, very well. Are you hurt?" He asked with empathy when he saw Daniel clutching his shoulder.

"Don't worry about it, I'll be fine. So what's next?"

"Mr. Fleischer is off to Central and we should take him before he wakes up. He is really quite a large oaf." Gales looked at Daniel with a newly formed admiration. He had already grown found of him as a man, and now, judging by what he had done to Fleischer, he could count on him in a pinch.

"William", Daniel grabbed Gale's arm and took him out of earshot of the others. "I know I haven't been here very long, but I like these people and would like to see them again. Is that possible?"

"Do you mean all of these people or just that person?" Gale pointed to Sharon as she joined them.

"If you want to join me, I'll be in Heaven for quite awhile. You should be able to find me easily." She smiled as she handed a piece of paper to Daniel.

Gale was already bending over Fleischer and before he could say anything they began to dematerialize. As he disappeared he could see Sharon mouth the words, "Thank you."

Central Booking was as crowded and chaotic as Daniel remembered. Penn Station on a Friday during rush hour would seem like a library in comparison. Of course at Penn Station people didn't vanish or appear at a moment's notice. Though some Guardians wore uniforms of some sort—probably what they wore when alive—most did not. "Hello, Mr. Lee", Daniel heard Gale say to the same holding officer they had met earlier. "Are you ready for the deportation?" They all looked down at the recovering Fleischer.

"Unfortunately Mr. Gale we are always ready for the deportations." Lee responded somewhat sadly. "Who is attending?"

"I think Mr. Lambert will attend this time." William then turned to Daniel and asked, if he wanted to go with Mr. Lee.

"Sure, I guess. Though I don't know what to do"

"Mr. Lee will instruct you. It is not very complicated but it is very intense so please prepare yourself." Daniel looked at Gale quizzically, but Gale turned to Lee and asked, "How long until you begin?"

"As soon as Fleischer wakes up we will begin."

Daniel became concerned. "I was lucky to get the upper hand on this brute. We might need assistance."

"Oh no Mr. Lambert, here in Central Holding, the bad guys have almost no strength at all. Even the giants such as Mr.

Fleischer can be controlled by someone as small as I am." He smiled and bowed very properly then vanished.

"People don't stick around in one place for very long. Do they?" Daniel asked rhetorically.

Gale answered anyway. "That's not true actually. People usually find an existence they are happy with and settle in for a long, long time. If I didn't have a job to do I would stay home with my Elizabeth and be fully content."

Assuming Elizabeth was Gale's wife Daniel was going to try to find out more about his partner's life—or death. But first enquired as to how long Mr. Lee would be.

"He'll be back when it's time. By the way Danny Boy I noticed that pretty young lady handed you a note before we left. Was it anything of import?" Daniel had forgotten about the note and Gale's knowing smile proved to Daniel that when it comes to men and women, things were the same no matter when one lived.

Opening the note Daniel saw the words Woolsthorpe Manor and was at a loss as to what they meant. "Maybe you can you make heads or tails of this," he asked Gale handing him the note.

"Woolsthorpe Manor. Of course I know, that is the birthplace of Sir Isaac Newton. He is, was, one of the greatest minds of all time." He said with Bristish pride. "Was he known in your time?"

"Newton, my God William, even in the 21st century, every high school physics class included Newton's Laws. Why do you think Sharon wrote that down?"

"Sharon, hey? Well Danny Boy, it may be measured in centuries since I last courted a young lady but it seems to this crusty old copper that Miss Sharon wants you to meet her at Newton's birthplace."

Daniel became a little flustered. "It's so vague there is no time or any instructions."

"Don't worry about that, when you are finished here just think yourself to meet Sharon at Woolsthorpe Manor. Heaven will take care of the rest and remember there is no time in heaven. I can't even begin to know how it all works; maybe you can ask Mr. Newton if you see him. Have a grand time and I'll see you when we are next called. Just wait for Mr. Lee." With that Gale was gone.

Trusting what Mr. Lee had told him, Daniel was not concerned as Fleischer struggled to his feet. His nose was no longer broken and he seemed none the worse for the beating he took. The healing must take a few minutes Daniel thought, and that's why Fleischer stayed unconscious for a little while and that was probably the reason for the time lag between when Gale and Jaffee left Dachau, to when they returned. Of course Daniel had no idea if there had even been a time lag and any conclusion he made about existence in Heaven was really just a guess.

"Don't try anything here, Fleischer," Daniel said sternly, "you have no strength here and you are already in enough trouble as it is." Eternal Damnation did seem like a lot of trouble to Daniel.

"Fuck you Jew lover", Fleischer spat on the ground as he spoke. Daniel could feel the man's hatred but couldn't understand it. The anger-one of the seven deadly sins as explained by Mac, Daniel remembered-was as palpable as a drum beat, though a lot less appealing.

"Follow me Mr. Lambert, and bring Mr. Fleischer with you," came the unflappable voice of Mr. Lee. Daniel saw him standing a few feet away then he turned and began to walk away.

"Let's go," Daniel reached up to grasped Fleischer's arm. He felt him trying to struggle but he was, as promised, powerless to resist. Walking quickly he caught up to Lee who seemed oblivious to all the commotion around them. Here is a man focused on his job, Daniel thought as he stumbled when Lee turned into a different corridor.

He heard Fleischer laugh and wondered for how much longer he would be able to laugh. The passageway was now empty and it was the ambient light that was changing from bright white to a redder tint as they walked. Daniel also began to notice an incredibly retched stench coming from the direction they were walking.

The most incredible shriek Daniel had ever heard caused him to pause. It seemed to go on and on and Daniel knew that something very bad was going happening to cause someone that much anguish. "Keep up please," Lee said sternly, his gait remaining unchanged. He did see a glint of fear in Fleischer's eyes as well as an ineffective hesitation in his walk. Daniel sensed that the brute was beginning to realize that he wasn't getting out of this one. *Fleischer is, literally and figuratively a dead man walking*, Daniel thought. Daniel wondered, and hoped, that Fleischer was feeling the fear that his victims felt as he led them to their deaths. This truly was and eye for an eye.

The foul odor was now almost too much for Daniel to bear and Fleischer was beginning to gag and his eyes now were wide open with terror. It was the smell of evil and it was unlike anything Daniel had ever experienced. It was worse than the body he had found in a missing person case. And that poor soul had been putrefying for days in 100-degree heat. Gauging from Fleischer's reaction it may even have been worse than the smell he helped to create in the concentration camp during his life.

Walking in the opposite direction Daniel saw an incredibly tall black man dressed in a red robe carrying a walking stick. His arms were festooned with golden wristbands and his face was heavily tattooed. His walk was straight and dignified and Daniel couldn't help nodding in respect.

Daniel had to pull up quickly as Mr. Lee stopped suddenly in front of him. "That scream you heard was Kamaria's deportation," He said motioning to the black man. "Mr. Kamaria is, like me, a Holding Officer, he was a Massi warrior of some renown when he lived. We are next so please be patient."

As they waited Daniel contemplated everything that had occurred since his death. He had no idea how long he had been in Heaven. He was starting to understand that time means very little to one's existence in Heaven—well short term such as hours or minutes might—but it was apparent that years, months, weeks and maybe even days had no bearing what so ever. It also dawned on him that he hadn't eaten anything and felt no hunger. He did drink a beer but hadn't felt thirsty at all. He hadn't noticed any bathrooms so he felt pretty sure that those functions were no longer required. He couldn't figure out how the whole timing thing worked. There were infinite numbers of times that a reality existed so how did one pick the correct time. Gale seemed to imply that that didn't matter you simply thought it and it happened. He hoped that was true, he did want to see Sharon again. *Do people fall in love in heaven?* He wondered.

Daniel was almost getting used to the smell; at least he was gagging less, when a grayish and very acrid smoke suddenly enveloped him. He could see through the haze but he subconsciously held his breath—not wanting to breathe it in. When he did he wished he hadn't. He saw that Fleischer was also hacking. Lee, on the hand, was as calm and peaceful as ever and Daniel wondered if anything could faze that man. As he began to regain his composure Daniel realized that the three men were no longer alone. He could not see anyone (or anything) else but his police sense told him that they were being watched.

The smoke cleared and Daniel looked up at Fleischer whose eyes were open as wide as possible. Turning to see what held Fleischer's attention Daniel saw what he could only say was some sort of demon.

It was naked and Daniel guessed that she was female (if demons had different sexes) from her lack of a penis and her apparent breasts, which were really just two saggy bags of skin hanging from her chest. Even though she was at least ten feet away he could smell her breath and it had the foul smell of decay and putrefying flesh. She had incredibly long and needle like finger and toenails. Which in turn were abnormally long and gnarled. Her hair was white. It was also thin and scraggly. Her eyes were completely red and her teeth were sharpened nubs. Over all she was the scariest and most hideous thing Daniel had ever seen.

Daniel was beyond surprised when he heard Mr. Lee calmly say, "Hello Hegate, I hope you are well?"

He was equally surprised when the demon responded. "Fuck you Lee you chink mother-fucker. I would like nothing better then to rip your slanted eyes out of your head and stuff them up your fucking ass." Her voice was raspy and yellow spittle flew from her mouth as she spoke.

Lee shook his head with pity. "Be that as it may, Hegate, I would like to present Daniel Lambert, a new Officer who has just joined us." He then turned to Daniel and smiled. "Mr. Lambert, this is Hegate, a collection demon from Hell. You will see her often." Daniel hoped not.

"It seems like there's more and more of you shit heads. If Heaven needs so many officers it must be turning into Hell." She threw her head back and laughed. If you could call that shrieking laughter, Daniel thought. "Who is the big bastard?" she asked looking piercingly at Fleischer.

"This is August Fleischer and he has been condemned to Hell for all eternity, as you well know." Lee responded solemnly. Daniel turned back to Fleischer and saw that he was now completely naked he was also blubbering like a baby.

"Of course I know who it is you fucking idiot," Hegate

snarled. "I'm just dicking around with you." Daniel was surprised, not so much by her crudeness—what would you expect from a demon—but that her comments were modern. As if she sensed what he was thinking she smiled and, Daniel would have sworn, winked at him.

He was about to address her when Fleischer screamed, "No, please God, no! I'll change, I swear..."

Before he could finish Hegate was upon him. Two fingers from her left hand punctured Fleischer's eyes and her thumb jammed into his mouth. She held his head like a bowling ball and yanked it down with such incredible force Daniel heard the bones in his neck breaking. With her right hand she grabbed his crotch and Daniel saw blood explode from his private parts. She then lifted him over hear head like a professional wrestler and shrieked with glee. Her strength was incredible, it didn't seem as if she was straining at all as she held the giant above her. Fleischer tried to struggle but it was futile, her grip was unrelenting. The magnitude of what he was witnessing dawned on Daniel like an epiphany. This man was going to Hell to suffer an eternity of torment. Daniel had heard fire and brimstone speeches before, but this was real. Daniel could not imagine what awaited Fleischer when he got to Hell but an eternity of this kind of torment was beyond his comprehension. There was no disputing that Fleischer was as evil as they come, but as Daniel watched him writhe in physical pain and considered the mental anguish he must be experiencing as it dawned on him what was about to happen, the Police Officer actually felt some compassion for him.

Even if he wanted to intervene there was nothing he could do because just as those compassionate thoughts were forming, Hegate and her wretched charge disappeared.

The smoke cleared and Daniel realized that the horrible taste in his mouth was not just from the smoke. "That was the most distressing thing I've ever seen," he said to Lee.

"Yes, Mr. Lambert, I am still touched by every deportation," the inscrutable Mr. Lee responded. "But you must understand that every one that enters Heaven is told what to expect and what is expected. Those with evil in their souls who cannot change have no place here. God made it this way so there is no other way."

"I understand that, I truly do. I also realize that God gives everyone a second chance. Daniel paused a moment as the thoughts gelled in his mind. "When I was alive, death was always the ultimate ending. Of course I hoped there was an afterlife and now know that there is one. But it's a tough place to grasp and it is far from any Heaven I ever imagined."

"Mr. Lambert, I was a communist and an atheist," Lee said as they walked. "When I was reborn here I was actually quite happy that everything didn't end with death." Daniel couldn't really imagine Mr. Lee being anything but the languid Mr. Lee he felt he was beginning to know, and to like. "Almost all of my family, despite the communist rule, were devote Buddhists so once I found myself in Heaven I thought it would be as Buddha taught. He had said that Heaven is a temporary place where those who have done good deeds experience more sensual pleasures for a longer period than those who have not. He also said that Hell is another temporary place where evildoers experience physical and mental suffering. I now believe that these things are untrue."

"So you are not really sure about the eternity thing?" Daniel asked.

"Ask me when we reach eternity," Lee said with a smile. He continued, "Buddha also said that each person's heaven was their own. That is very close to what Heaven is like. Of course he said karma was what established your heaven. I know now that in Heaven one creates his or her own reality."

They were now at the end of the deportation corridor and Mr. Lee stopped and turned to Daniel. "Mr. Lambert, Heaven is not perfect, it is not even the utopia so many hope for. It is what you make of it, so please go make something of it." He patted Daniel on the arm in a fatherly manner. "Think yourself someplace interesting, go explore. You will know when you are needed." With that Mr. Lee vanished.

Reaching into his pocket Daniel pulled out the slip of paper and reread the words. Here I go, Daniel thought, Woolsthorpe Manor and Sharon Jaffe.

Chapter 7

Looking around at his new surroundings Daniel believed his first solo attempt at thought travel had been successful. The setting was rural and probably English. The house in front of him was not large or ornate. It had the look of a farmhouse and the chimneys on each end and wooden shingles were hints as to its era.

The sun was high and there wasn't a cloud in the sky—it was a beautiful spring like day. Daniel was feeling a little warm in his winter clothes so he thought a nice tweed suit would be fitting. Not ever having owned one Daniel tried to picture the kind of clothes he had seen in British movies. Nothing changed and it dawned on him that maybe you needed to have worn it in life to wear it in death. He wondered if the rule applied to other material things as well. Of course that rule, if it was a rule, definitely didn't apply to places. Daniel had never been to England during his life and until William had told him, he had never heard of Woolsthorpe Manor. As he contemplated these more esoteric aspects of *life* in Heaven he also had to deal with the mundane. Thinking up his Rugby shirt, blue jeans and hiking boots, Daniel immediately felt more relaxed. He was glad that he couldn't conjure up the tweed suit. He was sure that during his life he would have felt pretentious in that type of attire and just as sure he would feel the same now, during his death.

Daniel could not see any people where he was standing and not being the kind of person who could just shout out—he had never felt comfortable drawing attention to himself—he decided to stroll around the property.

Turning the corner to the right side of the house Daniel saw a man writing on the wall. That alone was very odd to Daniel but when, as Daniel approached, the man looked at him and said, "Good afternoon, sir," the voice was pleasant and welcoming. "Are you the gentleman that is to meet Miss Sharon?"

Taken a little aback Daniel paused a moment before responding. "Yes I am meeting Sharon. My name is Daniel Lambert." He extended his hand. The man hesitated for an uncomfortable length of time but eventually accepted Daniels handshake.

"I am sorry for being rude, but I lived during the great plague and I avoided most physical contact." *Here was a man who had a reason to be germ phobic*, Daniel thought. "My name is Isaac Newton and this is my home."

He had shoulder length curly, dark blonde hair. Though not classically handsome he had a face filled with character, square jaw, aquiline nose, and bright eyes that exuded intelligence. His was dressed in knee-length pants with white knee-high socks. His shirt was long-sleeved with a ruffled collar. Daniel assumed the clothes were appropriate for his time of life. "It is a pleasure to meet you Sir Isaac," Daniel said as he started to bow then stopped when he realized what he was doing. *I must be picking up some of Williams British etiquette*, Daniel thought. *But I have a long way to go.*

"Sharon will be out presently," Sir Isaac said as he turned back to his graffiti. Daniel recognized calculus symbols but had no idea what any of them meant. It was a little surprising to Daniel that the great Physicist was writing on the walls of his house. Daniel attributed it to the quirkiness of genius—something that never affected him. *Well maybe quirkiness, definitely not genius*, he thought.

Daniel could hear Sir Isaac speaking as he worked. "Leibniz may have been correct about God but I'll be dammed if his *differentials* were not born from my *fluxions*." Though Daniel didn't have the foggiest idea as to what Sir Isaac's words meant.

"Sir Isaac you should really let all of that go," Daniel heard a woman's voice and turned to see Sharon approaching. "Keep in mind that Mr. Lambert is a Guardian and you are very close excessive pride." She looked as beautiful as Daniel had remembered. "It is very nice to see you again Daniel."

"And I you," Daniel responded with a courtly bow, thinking that he had already bowed more in Heaven than he had in his whole time on Earth. Though it did seem the action fit this time and place. Sharon's eyes sparkled in the sunlight as she smiled at him.

"Sir Isaac, Victoria asked me to inform you that tea is ready."

"It seems that the niceties of life in Heaven are the same as those on Earth. Of course I have no humanity to serve here so I can enjoy those niceties with much more delight. Will you join us Mr. Lambert?" Sir Isaac said as he extended his arm to Sharon to escort her in.

"Thank you, Sir Isaac, I will." Daniel responded. He was beginning to feel nervous that he might be competing with Isaac Newton for Sharon's interest. *Great, he thought, my rough around the edges personality versus one of the greatest minds in history.*

The inside of Sir Isaac's home reminded Daniel of some of the buildings he had visited during a family vacation to Colonial Williamsburg—a recreation of an 18th century American city. Candles accentuated the sunlight coming through the windows and created a cozy ambience of a bygone era.

Sir Isaac led them into the dining room where an attractive middle-aged woman stood at the head of a table which was set with a tea service as well as sandwiches and various pastries. Sir Isaac introduced the woman as his companion Victoria Clark. Daniel said hello but was more concerned that no one heard his sigh of relief as he realized that he wasn't competing with Isaac Newton for Sharon's affection.

I must be getting used to Heaven, Daniel thought. *Here I am having tea with the man who discovered gravity and I am okay with it.*

As they ate the food that Victoria had put out—partaking in a tea was another first for Daniel—their conversation centered on their lives on Earth. Rather than the misanthropic egotist he had been made out to be by historians, Daniel found Sir Isaac to be amiable and considerate. Because he had never married and was very devout, many of his biographers felt he had lived his life as a celibate priest. The reality was that, though they had never married, Sir Isaac and Victoria had had a nearly life long relationship that now continued in death. She was the daughter of Woolsthorpe Manor's town apothecary,\ with whom Newton lived for a number of years. During that time their romance flourished. Mr. Clark had provided the first stimulus to Newton's interest in chemistry. Mr. Clark and Victoria had also encouraged Newton to continue his studies rather than take up the life of a country farmer. That alone was enough to earn them an important place in history.

"Sir Isaac," Sharon said "I am very interested in hearing what you have learned during your thirty generations in Heaven. Is there a new *Principia* in the works?"

Daniel was getting the feeling that he might be out-brained in this group, but at least he knew that *The Principia* was a book written by Newton in which he explained his theories of motion. Of course he had never read it.

"The things I wrote about on Earth were meant to advance my ideas and hopefully advance human knowledge and understanding" Sir Isaac explained. "As with all scientific advancement, my discoveries on Earth were built on the shoulders of giants. Here in Heaven there are no shoulders, just existence. You can exist with family and friends if you so desire or you can exist all by yourself on a mountaintop or deserted island. You can also visit any time or place in history. Of course absolute time does not exist in Heaven. I can't say *Meet me tomorrow* or *I'll see you in one hour*. But I can say *let us meet at Woolsthorpe Manor, a*s I believe Sharon said to you, Daniel." He continued but directed his words to Daniel. "All we have to do is think that destination and we will be there. Thinking a destination is the same as traveling to a destination was when we were living on Earth. Of course in my time it took much longer to travel than in your time. But here in Heaven it's the same for everyone, instantaneous travel."

"I understand the thinking is traveling aspect, Sir Isaac," Daniel said as he processed the information. "But if there is no time in heaven, how would we coordinate the time to meet?"

"Now the picture becomes somewhat muddled, Daniel. The laws, if they are laws, are best explained using Quantum Mechanics, which was discovered long after I had passed from my Earthly existence." He smiled, took a sip of tea and then continued. "A Mr. Einstein, a brilliant man who visited my home, explained it to me. We had some very lengthy and stimulating conversations"

"I should say you did, Isaac," Victoria interjected. "It was so stimulating I slept through most of it. More tea Sharon?"

"No, but thank you Victoria. The Tea is lovely"

"Was it Albert Einstein?" Daniel's astonishment was noticeable.

"Yes, Albert was his name and I gather you have heard of him."

"Like you, he was a fairly well known scientist," Daniel responded. "Of course I never really understood any of what he did. Though I have to be honest and say that the two of you caused many sleepless nights for many generations of students throughout history."

"Well for all those sleepless nights I do apologize. To be honest Daniel, Mr. Einstein's theories were pretty hard for me also. I like things straightforward and observable. The effects of gravity are observable. Motion is observable." Sir Isaac became contemplative and dreamy as he spoke. Realizing that he was drifting off he shook his head, cleared his throat, and continued. "But I digress. Let us see if I can answer your question about ones ability to meet up with someone in Heaven." He picked up his half filled teacup. "If I should drop this cup all of us here know the final result. Gravity would cause the cup to fall. The cup would shatter when it hit the ground and the tea would spill out. Correct?" He paused briefly but continued before anyone could respond. Daniel noticed that Victoria had a look of concern as if she was not sure if Sir Isaac would drop the cup or was just using it as a prop. She was obviously relieved when Sir Isaac continued.

"In realty, that result is actually only one of an infinite number of possible results. Another result is that the cup will fall back together with the tea in it. Now the probability of that result is so small as to be not even worth considering, whereas the first result has such a high probability that it is considered a forgone conclusion that it will occur."

"And that matters, how?" asked Daniel.

"That brings us back to the timing issue of you meeting Sharon. You both think yourselves to my house and presto you are both there. You think that you might not both be there at the same time; after-all there are an infinite number of time possibilities. But in reality there is only one possibility, which is the reality of you both meeting here and the probability of that occurring is 100%."

"This realty then becomes your common reality. The four of us exist in this common reality because each of us chooses to be in this common reality. Anyone of us could leave this reality for another at any time. No one can force another to be in a specific reality. Of course Guardians seem to be the excluded from that rule. I have no idea how, though I assume it's a power given by God, but Guardians can latch hold of a person's existence and force it into another reality." He looked at Daniel. "Am I correct, Daniel?"

"Well, I am not sure where the power comes from but I can definitely force a reality on another. I also don't know all of the limitations of this power." He gently took hold of Sharon's arm. "For example I would love to take Sharon sailing but I don't know if that is within the capabilities of my power."

Daniel saw Sharon smile and blush. She then said. "We did see Daniel's partner take my Grandfather to another reality in order to prevent him from dying." She went on to describe the events at Dachau, including Daniel's fight with Fleischer. He noticed that Sharon beamed with pride when both Sir Isaac and Victoria looked at Daniel with a new respect. Now it was his turn to blush.

"Amazing," said Sir Isaac. "On Earth there existed, I mean still exists, a commonality amongst all living things. Here in Heaven all commonality, or shared experience, only exists within a common reality. The same is true for time. Here in Heaven, I believe, time only exists within a reality. There is no universal and unstoppable forward movement of time as there was on Earth. Mr. Einstein was quite interested in time. He believed that no event on Earth could accurately be described without explaining place and time." He folded his napkin and stood up. "But being in a reality, time for us is passing and it is time for my nap." He then thanked Victoria and walked up the stairs.

Time for Daniel during his visit to Woolsthorpe Manor passed way too quickly. Though he didn't spend as much private time with Sharon as he would have liked, the conversations amongst the four of them were enjoyable and stimulating. He learned much about life in the 1600's from Sir Isaac and Victoria. From them he realized that the old adage of things being better in the good old days might not be completely true. Disease and death were constant elements of everyday life. In the developed world during Daniel's time on Earth a dry summer usually only led to brown lawns and higher produce costs. For the inhabitants of Earth when Sir Isaac lived drought meant famine and large-scale death by starvation. Daniel came to understand why religion, which really meant hope for a better existence, was such an integral part of society.

This had led to a discussion of religion. Daniel learned that Sir Isaac had been a very pious person who had studied the Bible and other religious works. His religious beliefs were not true, as he learned when he died. He had definitely been a fire and brimstone believer. Of course the reality was better than he had thought. The idea of God giving every soul a second chance with the knowledge that they were being judged, really appealed to Sir Isaac's sense of fairness. "I am very pleased that the harsh judgment of God as preached by the Earthly ministers of my time was not real and just something they used to keep people in line," Sir Isaac said.

"Well I have seen some fire and brimstone," Daniel responded and he went on to explain his encounter with Hegate.

"There is no excuse for anyone in Heaven to act badly and especially badly enough to warrant condemnation to Hell,"

Sharon said with very strong emotions. "On Earth we had to take what we were told about God on faith. Here there is no doubt."

"There always has been and always will be people who feel that no rules apply to them," Daniel said. "I've seen more than my fair share on Earth and now in Heaven."

The time flew by, at least time in this reality, and Daniel enjoyed every minute of it. One morning Daniel was looking out the window at an apple tree wondering if that was *the tree*, when Sharon came up behind him. "You might not be able to carry me off to your boat but I can certainly go of my own volition. If you ask nicely."

Daniel's voice cracked, "Would you like to go sailing Sharon... Please."

"I would love to." She responded with a smile that caused Daniel to become excited. Not in a lustful way, more because he wanted to share something he loved, sailing, with someone for whom his fondness was growing.

Daniel felt some sadness when they said good-bye and thank you to Victoria and Sir Isaac. They invited Daniel and Sharon to return anytime. Daniel hoped he would get an opportunity to return to this delightful couple. He turned to Sharon and said, "Think yourself to *Old Man Time* located in Sweden Point Marina on the Potomac River."

"*Old Man Time*, Sweden Point Marina, Potomac River," Sharon repeated as she took hold of Daniel's hand.

He never thought traveled hand-in-hand with Gale, Daniel thought as Woolsthorpe Manor and his new friends shimmered and disappeared. Though he knew it wouldn't be as nice as this.

Chapter 8

In the next instant he was at the helm of his beloved sailboat, *Old Man Time*, with the sails drawing nicely and a perfect heel as she plowed through the waters of the Potomac River. Even if he was completely blind he would still know the river on which he had spent so much time—and they were very happy times. The smell of aquatic vegetation decaying in the sun was all he needed to tell him where he was. He assumed most rivers might have that smell but just as a mother knew her babies aroma he knew his river's. That pungent *fishy* scent that some people found repulsive, Daniel found intoxicating and invigorating. The sights—a bird of prey roosting on a marker or a great blue heron hunting in the shallows—and the smells, represented life on the river. And it represented a time when he was most at ease. The exuberance he felt was increased even more when he saw Sharon sitting next to him. She was wearing white, calf high pants, white boat shoes and a blue lightweight windbreaker. Her outfit was very nautical, very 60's and very attractive.

The wind was fresh at about 20 miles per hour and was perfect sailing weather. Daniel loved it, but for non-sailors it could be disconcerting. Sailboats leaned over, heeled, because of the wind pressure on the sails. The higher the speed of the wind, the greater the pressure, the more the boat heeled over. *Old Man Time* was a heavy and very seaworthy 27-foot boat that could easily sail in winds twice as strong, though in deference to Sharon he spilled some of the wind off the sails to lessen the heel. He then turned the boat more down wind so the wind force acted more on pushing the boat forward and less on leaning it over.

"How are you doing," he asked Sharon who seemed a lot less tense now that the boat was more level.

"I'm fine Daniel. Though the last time I was on a boat it was on the S.S. United States sailing from France to New York and that one was a little bigger than this one." Daniel knew that the S.S. United States was one of the last of the real ocean liners. In her hey day during the 1950's she was the fastest passenger liner ever. She was one of the last of the grand ladies of the sea that were eventually replaced by quicker and cheaper—though less romantic—air travel. The only large passenger ships that remained after the departure of the ocean liners were the giant cruise ships. Most sailors worth their salt considered these behemoths to be more like floating hotels rather than real ships. The thought that he and Sharon might become close enough that he could relive that trip with her filled him with excitement. Excitement about the ship and about Sharon.

"You seem to really know what you are doing." Sharon said admiringly. Daniel welcomed the praise, which seemed genuine. He explained to her that he had grown up on this river, just a few miles north from where he was now, and had been a sailor for most of his life. He had started sailing when he was twelve. He had refinished an old boat that someone from the local marina had given him. It leaked, it was slow and a puff of wind could capsize it, but Daniel couldn't get enough. He sailed every day. By the time he was in high school Daniel had become an expert sailor. One day, to Daniel's surprise and delight, his father—more to appease Daniel than to broaden his horizons—purchased a 20-foot sailboat. It had been ostensibly for the family, but only Daniel used it. He actually could not remember a time when the whole family sailed together. Of course all of that was literally a lifetime ago.

Sharon listened attentively and Daniel became a little embarrassed but he felt compelled to try to get her to understand something that had been so important in his life—though he wasn't sure why. "Sailing has always been my escape," Daniel continued. "To me there is nothing as satisfying as harnessing the wind to control the movement of a two-ton vessel. When I'm sailing I have to be aware of everything, the weather, the boat, and other boats in the area. I have sailed her so many times that I know each sound. If I hear one noise that is out of place I am on alert. She is my body and I am the brain that controls it all."

Sharon let him go on; she sensed that he needed to plus his passion was infectious. He was desperately trying to connect the life he departed so suddenly with this new life, of which he did not yet understand. This was something she was also still trying to accomplish, even though she had been in Heaven for much longer than Daniel.

He told her that his goal throughout high school had been to attend the United States Naval Academy. He mentioned, with some sadness it seemed to Sharon, that he had to do it all on his own. His father provided zero guidance or help and his mother had no idea about goals or dreams. "Get married and raise a family," was the extent of her advice. When he wasn't accepted to the Academy he was devastated and he basically gave up. His senior year was one of drinking, partying and doing just enough schoolwork to graduate. "I fell in with a bad crowd, as they say," Daniel said. She watched with admiration, his obvious skill—

even to a novice as herself—as he adjusted this and moved that. His ability to handle the myriad of tasks and still keep talking was impressive.

Daniel stopped talking about himself; she sensed he had become self-conscious and began pointing out landmarks as the shoreline slipped by. It seemed to Sharon that they were alone in the universe. It was just the two of them, a boat and a river that never ended. Though she had known him only briefly, especially as compared to eternity—Sharon had never been so happy, in life or in death. "How did you get into police work?" She asked wanting to bring the conversation back to his life.

"They say you have to reach bottom before starting up again," he continued. "After my senior year I was caught breaking into a neighbor's house. Just for kicks. The policeman who caught me was from my neighborhood and also a sailor. He used to let me crew for him in the local races and he seemed to think I was a pretty good sailor. But even though I thought we were friends that didn't stop him from handcuffing me and tossing me in his squad car. But to my surprise he took me to our marina, not to jail. To this day I remember his words, 'Daniel, you have an important choice facing you right now. You can stay on this course, but believe me dangerous waters lay ahead. Or you can come about and steer your ship of life on a course that will lead to a productive and fulfilling voyage.' He then took off my handcuffs asked me to get out and drove away. That was it. He never mentioned the incident again and I still don't know how he covered it up. Within a few days I enrolled in a law enforcement program, became a cop, got married, had a daughter, got divorced, got shot, and died. I guess that was productive and fulfilling."

"It sounds like it was," Sharon said trying to counter the sarcasm in his voice, by agreeing with him. You obviously had time to buy this boat and you can't convince me that your daughter wasn't fulfilling."

"You're right, and I'm sorry. My life was not really that bad. Especially compared to what you and so many others went through. I loved, I mean love, my daughter and she is, believe it or not, the only person I miss. But that's it, I'm done." Sharon watched as Daniel suddenly became a bundle of motion. He turned the boat so that the sails were flapping. The boat slowed dramatically. He scrambled to the front of the boat and dropped the anchor. He then lowered the sails. After making everything *shipshape* as he said, he sat down across from her.

"Here we are," he said.

"And where would here be, pres tell?" She asked coyly.

"Do you see that house in the distance?" He pointed towards the shore. Following his gaze Sharon could see a white mansion up a hill and overlooking the river.

"That's Mt. Vernon, where George Washington lived." She exclaimed as she recognized the house. "I visited it when I was in college, before you were born, young man." She gently put her hand on Daniel's hand. He slowly tilted his head and leaned towards her. Sharon knew that they were about to kiss and she was looking forward to it. She had looked forward to it from the time she had met him. In life she had never trusted men, at least not since that fateful night in Germany. It was different with Daniel. She felt safe with him and he was so damn handsome.

She was pretty sure where the kissing would lead. This thought was confirmed when he stood and led her to the cabin. "Watch your step, this is no ocean liner. It's not even an ocean liner's lifeboat."

The cabin was cute, at least it seemed so to her. All of life's necessities were here though more compact. She could stand upright but Daniel had to hunch over to avoid hitting his head. "It's adorable, Daniel, like a playhouse."

He laughed. "I never heard it called that before. I always thought of it as efficient and nautical."

"Like its owner, right?"

"You know Sharon; I was attracted to you as soon as I met you. It's not just a physical attraction, it's like I just want to be with you. Talk, share experiences. Do you know what I mean?" She sensed that how she answered this question was very important to him. It was as if he had let down his defenses and was ready for a blow to the face or a hug.

She decided to give him the metaphorical hug he desired. "I feel the same. As a matter of fact I have never, in life or death felt this way."

He pulled her toward him and they kissed, much more passionately than before. He led her to a small cabin in the front of the boat. The bed in the cabin took up almost all of the available space, coming to a point at the front. *What had Daniel called the front? Bow, that was it,* she remembered. Trying to remember nautical names did not diminish the passion she felt for Daniel.

Their lovemaking was not like anything Sharon remembered from her life. The two times she had had sex she had been in her early twenties and they were clumsy, groping efforts by boys who, she now realized, knew very little about true lovemaking.

Daniel's caresses were tender and compassionate. She felt that he sensed that she was inexperienced and a little frightened. When they had both climaxed he didn't just roll over like a sated lion, he held her tight in a loving embrace. He whispered in ear that she was beautiful and he was so glad that they had met. They were two souls who were now joined in eternity, for eternity. She had no doubts about this and she now felt that she was truly in Heaven.

They spent days in this wonderful reality. They would sail for hours each day. The destination didn't matter; the joy was in the voyage. Daniel patiently taught her how to sail. She was a quick learner, probably because she wanted to feel the same delight for sailing that he felt. Every evening they would anchor in an idyllic creek off the main channel. His galley was stocked as he had stocked in life. Though they didn't need to eat or drink, they did so for the pleasure and for the camaraderie. She was really relieved that the baser bodily functions were not a requirement in Heaven—especially in the cramped quarters of *Old Man Time*.

"When I was alive I always said, now it's *back to reality*, whenever a sailing trip was over," he said to her one evening as the sat in the cockpit of the boat, enjoying the fresh night air. "Now I don't know what is real. Is there such a thing as yesterday or tomorrow anymore? I do know that I would like this to continue as long as possible." He put his arm around her as he said this.

He asked her what part of life she missed most and she couldn't really think of anything she missed at all. "I had a pretty boring life," she responded. "I had always hoped Heaven would be better and it is." He smiled at her lovingly as she said this.

He asked her with all sincerity if she had been able to figure *this whole Heaven thing out*. Some of the contradictions bothered him such as "where the hell are all the people?" He asked as he pointed to the empty river. "My greeter, Mac, had told me over a trillion people had died and since I've been dead I have seen a few thousand, at thee most."

During the time that she had lived, men rarely deferred to women on any discussions with a scope beyond home and hearth. She had earned a PhD in Societal Anthropology from Dalhousie University, yet her ideas had often been dismissed as flighty girl thoughts. Many of the men who had been so dismissive were not even close to being Sharon's intellectual equal. Daniel was different, maybe it was the time and place he had lived, maybe it was just the way he was. But she knew he respected her opinions and he was now reaching out to her to help him understand this new existence.

"I don't think we can ever truly understand Heaven," She said. "We can never forget that God created it and though it's not the perfect Heaven so many envisioned, it is what he created. So, just as we can never truly know God, we can truly never know Heaven."

"I do know that it is vastly different than life on Earth. Jean-Paul Sartre was a philosopher and writer who said that *existence precedes essence.* The philosophy was called existentialism." She hesitated not wanting to sound pompous.

Daniel smiled, sensing her thoughts. "Don't worry Sharon, I want to learn and there is little doubt that you are the smartest person in this boat, and the best looking."

"You are such a sweet talker, Mr. Lambert, you may just have your way with me," she said coyly. She continued, "Sartre was also an atheist so even though his religious beliefs were wrong, the phrase *existence precedes essence,* is true. Our life on Earth was our existence, which preceded our life in Heaven, our essence."

Sharon observed that Daniel was absorbing the information as she spoke. She saw that he was looking back at her with rapt attention. "On Earth," she continued, "Humans are mostly concerned with bodily existence. But, and this is important, how they exist is fundamental to the formation of their essence. When we die our essence lives on in Heaven, with the only caveat being that we must live by the rules God established..."

"The seven virtues," Daniel interrupted. "It's my job as a Guardian to make sure we live by those virtues and from what I've seen not everyone can or even wants to." He became very contemplative. "The complexity of ruling over the billions of souls seems beyond impossible."

"We are talking about God, Daniel." Sharon said. "Additionally, on Earth we lived as humanity, a society of billions. Here we live as individuals. There is no society, No commonality of existence except existence itself. And to answer your question, there are an infinite number of existences and that's why Heaven is not packed full of people."

"I guess that the old adage 'you are born alone and die alone' is very accurate. Of course it doesn't mean that you have to be dead alone." This thought pleased both of them and together they stood up and headed into the cabin.

The next morning as Daniel sat drinking his coffee, waiting for Sharon to wake he was startled to hear the sound of boat engine. Hustling on deck he saw a large and very powerful motorboat bearing down on them. When he had lived he couldn't even afford the gas for a monster like that, much less the monster itself. He guessed that gas just like food was perpetual here in Heaven. He wondered if those powerful boats caused environmental pollution in Heaven. On Earth they were called *stink potters*; at least that's what sailors called them. Of course motor boaters called sailors *rag baggers*. Probably not, he thought, considering that unlike Earth there was not a single environment, there were an infinite number, as Sharon had pointed out.

He saw two men in the boat and his life-learned tendency to be suspicious of everyone kicked in. Sharon stuck her head out the cabin entrance, "Is there someone else here?" To answer her Daniel pointed toward the boat which inexplicably continued towards them.

Sharon appeared to become concerned. "In all likelihood they're just curious," he said reassuringly. "But just in case I have an equalizer attached to the bulkhead next to you." Sharon poked her head back in the cabin and came out holding a wooden nightstick. "Speak softly and carry a big stick," she said as she handed the weapon to Daniel.

By this time the strangers had come alongside *Old Man Time.* The appearance of the men did nothing to lessen Daniel's apprehension. Both men, one white and one black, wore t-shirts that did little to conceal their muscular physiques. They stared at Daniel as if appraising his strength. The look they gave Sharon made Daniel shudder.

Without warning the driver gunned the powerful dual engines of his boat. The roar was deafening. He then turned the boat hard to the right causing the back of the boat to smash into the side of *Old Man Time* with a sickening crunch. The sailboat lurched sideways and the force caused Daniel to briefly lose his footing. He saw Sharon fall backwards into the cabin landing with a sickening thud. "Are you all right?" he shouted over the roar of the engines. When Sharon didn't respond Daniel leapt down into the cabin. She was just starting to stand. "Sharon, are you hurt?" He asked as he helped her up.

"I'm fine Daniel. What was that about?"

"That's a question I can't answer. Though I do know that wasn't a friendly *howdy do.*" Their smiles belied their anxiety as they thought about their next step. "We have to leave this reality just in case they come back." Sharon said. Sensing his trepidation she continued. "Don't worry about the boat, Daniel. Once we leave, this reality is gone forever from our existence. We can visit *Old Man Time* by just creating a new reality."

"Of course, we'll leave this reality to those punks." As he was asking Sharon where she wanted to go, Daniel felt a small bump. *Fuck,* he thought. *They're back and I wasn't paying attention. Fuck, fuck, fuck.* With his strong compunction for instant action Daniel jumped through the cabin door when the smart think would have been for the two of them to just disappear. He then realized he had made his second mistake when he turned around after leaving the cabin. Standing on the cabin roof, directly above him, Daniel saw the black man from the boat. It was too late to do anything. The man's heavy motorcycle boot was already in full motion. Daniel tried to protect his face but the boot connected with the side of Daniel's head. As he fell Daniel fought hard not to lose consciousness. The ringing in his head was deafening but his instincts were still functioning. He spun his body and extended his forearm in a defensive position. Just in time. Assailant number two was swinging a wooden boat oar at full speed. The pain in Daniel's arm told him that his bone had shattered. Better his forearm than his skull he thought. His appraisal of the situation was not encouraging. It was now two muscle-bound bad guys against a bell wrung, one-armed former cop. The odds became a little more even when Daniel saw Sharon emerge wielding Daniel's nightstick. Catching one of the assailants by surprise, she jabbed the nightstick directly into his kidney. Capitalizing on the moment of surprise, Daniel smashed his fist into the testicles of the second bad guy. He gasped then doubled over in the classic 'hit in the balls' pose. Getting ready to deliver the knockout blow, Daniel noticed that assailant number one had recovered enough from the kidney blow to grab hold of Sharon's shoulder. Redirecting his attention Daniel started toward them. At first he thought his vision had blurred from the head kick when Sharon and the bad guy began to shimmer.

"NO," he screamed as he realized what was happening. Before he had finished shouting and before they had completely disappeared Daniel head butted the assailant in the stomach. He wasn't sure what happened when you interrupted a conveyance, and he didn't care. He just knew that he had to stop this guy from taking Sharon. The force of Daniels head hitting the man's stomach achieved the desired affect. There had been some kind of rope, or something, around Sharon's arm and as the man let go of the end Sharon stopped disappearing. The bad guy, on the other hand, vanished. Of course when he disappeared so did his stomach which had been acting as a backstop to Daniel's head as he charged. With the forward momentum now completely unobstructed—and as Sir Isaac had stated; *a body in motion tends to stay in motion*—Daniel fell through the cabin door and came to rest nearly halfway towards the bow of the boat. Ignoring his pain Daniel recovered his composure enough to get back on deck, grasp Sharon's shoulder and thought, *Central Holding.*

Chapter 9

As soon as he acclimated to his new location, Daniel's head cleared and any injuries he sustained on the boat were gone. He was relieved to see Sharon next to him.

"This is Central Holding; it's where we bring chronic offenders." He said as he noticed her looking around.

"It's quite a busy place," she said soaking in the bedlam that was Central Holding. "I didn't realize that there were so many offenders in Heaven. Is it always this busy?"

"I don't know if it's always this busy but every time I come here it's like this." He hadn't given the business much thought until now. It seemed incongruous that Heaven's lock-up (and that's what it was) should be so full of activity.

"Greetings Mr. Lambert," Daniel was surprised to hear the ever-courteous Mr. Lee. "Where is Mr. Gale? It's very unorthodox for a member of a Guardian team to bring an offender in by himself." Mr. Lee looked at Sharon as he spoke.

"Oh no Mr. Lee, I am not here on official business. Sharon and I," he motioned toward Sharon, "were sailing when two thugs in a powerboat attacked us. One of them grabbed hold of Sharon and was transporting her to I don't know where. I had to act fast and the only place that came to mind was here. So here we are."

Mr. Lee looked down and shook his head. "Though not common, I have heard of similar incidents. I must admit that it seems to be happening more and more and I don't have any explanation as to why." He then looked up at Sharon and with genuine concern and said, "Well I hope you are both fully recovered from your ordeal." Sharon and Daniel acknowledged that they were both okay then Daniel formally introduced Sharon and Mr. Lee.

Mr. Lee, why is it that you are always here whenever I or Bill and I arrive?"

"The answer to why is simple," Mr. Lee responded. "I am assigned to the two of you, so whenever you are here I am also. That is the why, Mr. Lambert, but I don't know the *how*."

"It's like being on call, all the time." Sharon interjected. Daniel was very impressed with how perceptive she was. "It must be a little discombobulating not knowing when you'll be called."

"Not really Miss Sharon. I believe, though I'm not completely sure, that because time does not cross realities, my summoning here always comes when I am ready. God has set this up so that time can compress or expand in one reality in order to synchronize with another reality, if needed." He smiled at Sharon, which impressed Daniel—he had a strong feeling that Mr. Lee doled out smiles sparingly. "Of course don't ask me how it works; I am but a humble servant of Heaven."

"That's all well and good, but there doesn't seem to be anyway for us humble servants to share information with other humble servants," Daniel said discouragingly. "These attacks may be happening all over the place but since no central information center exists Guardians can't compare notes with other Guardians. Am I correct in surmising this?"

"You are absolutely correct, Mr. Lambert. We are not a police force. We may operate in small groups, but that is it. We do not investigate, we do not coordinate with others, we do not compare notes, as you say, and we have no knowledge of our assignments until that knowledge is divinely inputted into our brains."

"But that seems so inefficient," Daniel responded. He wanted to say more but Mr. Lee interrupted.

"Remember, Mr. Lambert, Heaven is not a society or a nation or even a world. It is a place created by God. He created Heaven as a place where humans exist but in reality it is only our souls that exist here. We do not need food, water or air to breath. We don't have to worry about bills, about war, about any of the things we needed to worry about on Earth." He paused and looked at Daniel and Sharon as a father would look at his child. "Everyone that arrives in Heaven is told without any ambiguity how they must act. If they choose to behave in ways that violate the rules of Heaven they are made to leave. Unfortunately, vast numbers think that they can act in Heaven as they did on Earth and that Mr. Lambert and Miss Sharon is why this place exists." With a swirl Mr. Lee pointed out Central Booking, which continued to be, Daniel noted, as busy as ever.

It was at that moment that Daniel realized he was receiving an assignment. The notification was not like an epiphany or any kind of mystical revelation. He just knew.

Ushirka Yamoto, a very successful Japanese businessman who had worked hard and played hard. He was an avid mountain climber and had climbed some of the highest peaks in the world. Unfortunately he never made it to the summit of the highest and he died on Mt Everest during his seventh attempt at reaching the summit. His obsession with summiting never left him, even upon his death, and the fact that he can't reach the top is adversely impacting his existence and thusly his soul. He had always considered himself a top notch mountaineer and this vanity concerning his climbing ability is clouding his judgment. Even in death he continues to pursue his vainglorious goal of conquering Everest. Current location is a tent 2,000 feet below the summit of the mountain.

Just as his assignment became clear Daniel noticed his partner appearing. As Gale came into view Daniel burst out laughing. "What the hell? You look like a Swiss Yodeler."

The surprise at seeing Gale not in his uniform was greatly surpassed by the surprise in what he was wearing. Gale was dressed in an old fashioned Tyrolean mountain outfit. Wool knickers and jacket, knee-high socks and a feather in his wool cap. "May I enquire as to what is so funny," Gale asked, a little annoyed. "I am dressed in mountaineering suit for a mountain assignment. I presume you'll be wearing short pants and a short sleeved shirt?"

Ignoring Daniel, Gale turned to Sharon and tipped his hat. "It is nice to see you again Sharon. May I ask why you are here?"

"Daniel and I had some trouble and the best escape was coming here."

Gale looked quizzically at Daniel, who was now dressed in his warmest ski outfit from his life. The *ensemble* included long underwear, water and wind resistant jacket and pants, gloves, hat and hiking boots. "I'll tell you about it later," Daniel said to Gale in response to his unasked question. He turned to Sharon. "Where can I meet you when we are finished?"

"Meet me at my home in Halifax." Sharon responded. She then kissed him on the cheek and was gone.

Gale gave Daniel a sly nod and then Central Booking began to shimmer and disappear.

The wind and cold hit Daniel like a sledgehammer. The shock caused him to take a deep breath. He immediately knew that this was a mistake. The cold air filled his lungs and it felt as if he had swallowed bricks. His chest felt heavy and he became lightheaded. His body was screaming at him that it wasn't getting enough air. Though his brain was addled he realized that they must have landed somewhere on Mt. Everest. The cold, the wind and the lack of oxygen was way too severe for the skimpy clothes they were wearing. He saw that Gale was also struggling. "We are going to die right here if we don't do something," he shouted to Gale. The effort it took just to shout exhausted Daniel. The more he gasped for air the more it felt as if he was suffocating. They both new they wouldn't last five more minutes. He was about to shout that they should go back to Central when Gale pointed. Right in front of them like an oasis in the desert was the very recognizable outline of a tent. Being the nearest Daniel unzipped the flap—he was surprised he found the zipper so easily-scrambled in and then helped Gale enter. Just being out of the wind was a vast improvement and it became even better when Daniel realized that the temperature was just cold and not mortally cold. It was still hard to breath but at least it didn't hurt when he did so.

"Hello gentlemen. It doesn't seem like a very nice night for a stroll."

Daniel looked up and sitting at the back of the tent next to a small portable lamp was Ushirka Yamoto. He had a cup of steaming something held in both hands, his smile visible behind the vapor coming from the cup. "Would you like a cup of tea?" He asked with a slight bow of his head.

"Thank you and yes," said Gale still blowing in his hands, trying to warm them up.

The relative coziness of the scene in the tent seemed extremely tenuous considering that all that separated them from the tempest outside was a few millimeters of fabric. As Yamoto poured the hot tea Daniel expected the tent to be ripped to shreds at any moment.

Not wanting to remain here any longer than necessary, Daniel decided to do away with any pretense of courtesy. "Ushirka Yamoto, you are in violation of the sin of Pride. We are here to insist that you stop this behavior and return to a Heavenly existence that conforms to the laws of Heaven." *How fucking weird was that,* Daniel thought as he finished his ad homonym admonishment.

Not phased at all Yamoto took another sip, savored it and said, "I have always admired the way Americans could do away with formalities and get right to the point." He looked at Daniel, "I am correct, you were an American in life?"

Daniel nodded.

"Well I truly appreciate the effort and risk you are making on my behalf. I will admit I am obsessed with reaching the top of this mountain. When I died, on my seventh attempt, I was literally minutes away. But I couldn't go on, I could not lift my feet to walk, I could not work my radio. All I could do was sit in the snow and watch and shiver. I watched and shivered as climbers went by on their way to the summit. I watched and shivered as they returned from the summit. I watched and shivered as they shouted words I could not understand into my face. I watched and shivered as they talked amongst themselves. I knew that they wanted to help but I also knew that any rescue attempt was impossible. Anyone who climbed this high on Everest knew this. I watched and shivered as the last climber disappeared. I watched and shivered as the sun vanished, and then suddenly I stopped shivering and I just watched. When the wind finally stopped blowing and the snow settled it had covered me up to my head but I could see the stars above me and I seemed so close to them that I felt that if I could just move my arms I could reach one. Of course I couldn't move my arms so I just watched them. After a while, I don't know how long, I stopped watching and closed my eyes. As I did so I felt as if the mountain, the gracious victor, now welcomed me, the vanquished foe, into its arms. And then I died."

Gale, who had wrapped himself in a sleeping bag, seemed touched by the story. Always courteous he said, "Mr. Yamoto, your efforts to reach the top were probably considered valiant in life. Here in Heaven your continuing pursuit of this obsession is becoming prideful. What's worse is that you are risking your eternal existence."

"I presume you mean I risk damnation to hell."

"Not really, Mr. Yamoto, my partner means you risk dying, again." Daniel added, "And there is no guidance or hints as to what comes next."

"I didn't really know what came next when I lived," Yamoto responded. "By I do know that my very strong desire to reach the summit has transcended my life into my death. To this point I have always managed to transport out of danger so I should be fine"

"Not if a rock hits your head," Gale said sternly. "You said you tried seven times in life to reach the top. How many attempts have you made since dying?" Gale asked.

Yamoto thought for a second. "About fifty," he replied and his answer was tinged with embarrassment. "As a matter of fact I thought maybe I was in hell and I had been condemned to try over and over for eternity. Like Sisyphus from western mythology pushing the rock up the hill.

"Unlike Sisyphus, you have a choice. We are here to strongly," Daniel emphasized strongly, "advise you to consider another path."

As the storm buffeted the tent Daniel felt oddly content sitting in their little cocoon. Though far from warm the three of them were generating enough body heat to make it tolerable. It was still hard to breath and he was beginning to get a headache.

"Are we at risk being this high up?" he asked Yamoto.

"Yes, because you are not acclimating to these high altitudes you are suffering from AMS, acute mountain sickness. You get a headache fairly quickly but serious symptoms don't normally show up for twelve hours."

"What are those serious symptoms?" Gale asked.

"Vomiting, brain embolism, and death." Yamoto responded with a smirk. "It doesn't really matter because at this height we are in the death zone and eventually anyone who stays too long will die."

"That cinches it, we should go," Daniel said with authority and began to make his way towards Yamoto.

"Gentlemen, I understand that you are enforcing the laws of heaven—a noble and honorable endeavor." Yamoto bowed slightly. "But I hope and humbly ask that you indulge me one more attempt. I will leave now and return immediately upon summiting or if I become sure that I would make it to the top."

Daniel looked at Gale for counsel.

"We do have some discretion on matters such as this," Gale said. "Mr. Yamoto is not endangering anyone else…"

"Except us."

"Well yes that is true but if we stay here I don't believe the risk is that great," Gale saw Yamoto nod in affirmation. "I think one more try will be fine but, I want your promise that if you make it or not this is the last attempt for awhile."

"You have my promise and my gratitude."

With that Yamoto was up. The two Guardians watched with interest as Yamoto prepared for his final attempt. Before putting on his oxygen mask Yamoto said, "Thank you both again. It will take me approximately seven hours to summit. Because I do not have to trek back I won't need to conserve my oxygen supply." He pointed out the two extra Oxygen tanks in his pack. In his pack Daniel notice a small Japanese flag. Noticing his look Yamoto said, "I know this is not real, but I thought I would make it as real as possible by planting this flag. I also have a picture of my father to place at the summit. His whole life he toiled to make life better for his family. He never once did anything for himself. But he did dream and he dreamt of these mountains most of all…"

Yamoto could not continue and turned his face away. With some sadness Daniel compared his own disdain for his father with Yamoto's obvious respect. "Is your father still alive?" Gale asked.

"No, Mr. Gale, he passed away twenty years before I did. He actually never saw any of my attempts on Mt. Everest."

"That's another reason to tow the line in Heaven," Daniel took this last opportunity to stress to Yamoto why they were here. "You should be able to find your father and tell him of your adventures. I'm sure he would be very proud of your effort to fulfill yours and his dreams."

Yamoto nodded then attached his facemask without saying a word. Daniel reasoned that one of the reasons Yamoto was so determined to summit was that he wanted to be able to tell his father that he had. The cold and wind filled the tent instantly as Yamoto entered the darkness to finish a quest that he began in life and which carried over into his death. Like Don Quixote he would attack his windmill one more time and Daniel wished him success.

Gale watched Daniel as he secured the tent flaps after Yamoto's departure. Gale felt that Daniel was different than other modern police officers he had met. Many were brooding and cynical, whereas Daniel carried himself with dignity and was extremely courteous—His earlier berating of Yamoto notwithstanding. If Gale was cynical himself, Daniel's demeanor might make him suspicious—but he wasn't and Gale had grown attached to the young man since they had become partners.

"I hope he makes it this time," Daniel said to Gale as he fumbled with the alcohol stove. "Would you like some tea?"

"Yes thank you. I guess we have about seven hours to wait." Gale wrapped himself in the sleeping bag as if he were a bear preparing for a long hibernation.

As the two Guardians sipped their tea a sense of calmness enveloped the tent and they both became contemplative. Daniel was the first to break the lethargic silence.

"If the truth be told, William, I find Heaven somewhat disturbing."

"And why is that Danny Boy?"

"Well first of all there is the sense that people don't really change after death. The slate is not really wiped clean with death, so however you were in life carries over into heaven. I don't think it's a true second chance."

Gale did the best he could in explaining that though people carry there personality traits over into death, the rules are explained to all and in that sense all are given the same chance.

"Think about this Daniel, in life a vast majority of crimes or bad behavior results from need or circumstance. Victor Hugo was a French poet of some renown who lived in my time."

"I've heard of him, William. He wrote *Les Misérables,* which was turned into successful Broadway play."

"I find it interesting that his story spanned so many generations. I read his novel the last year of my life and I've read it numerous times since then. In the story Jean Valjean is sent to prison for five years for stealing food for his starving family. He wasn't a bad man, he stole out of need. In Heaven he would not have that need and a man such as Jean Valjean would have a fine existence. Not one of the seven sins of Heaven, not one," Gale repeated for emphasis, "is related to need. They all are based on excessive or unnatural wants. Whether it's Fleischer and his viscous hatred of Jews or the very pleasant Mr. Yamato and his excessive desire to climb this mountain, in Heaven they are all the same. But Danny Boy I have never sent a violator to Hell for anything but the worst transgressions. And even they usually get a warning or two."

The sun was now shining and though still cold, Gale could feel a slight warming from its light. He tried to think of a way to get Daniel to understand that just because his preconceived ideas as to what Heaven was were not accurate, it wasn't less than what God intended—it was exactly what got intended.

"Danny Boy, you are trying too hard to make Heaven what you want it to be instead of accepting it for what it is. It is Heaven where we are judged by God. How we live here is what determines our eternity."

"I get that, but what I don't understand is why God, whoever the hell he is, doesn't free us from all of our Earthly baggage when we die."

"Just because we don't understand doesn't make it wrong. And if you think about it we are freed of much of our Earthly burdens when we die." Gale thought for a moment then asked, "What parts of your existence on Earth tried your spirit the most?"

"I don't know…there was so much."

"Just say the ones that pop right into your mind."

"Okay. War, terrorism, corruption, greed, selfishness, traffic, over-population, crime, drugs, for a start," Daniel said.

"Not much different than my time," Gale responded. "It

seems that each time had good and bad attributes. But here in Heaven, the societal factors are gone. There are no governments to make war, or levy taxes; and no corrupt leaders to benefit from war and taxes; there is no over-population, or foul smelling rivers filled with human waste and trash." Gale thought for a moment about the Thames River of his life. "If you ask me it really is not as bad as you perceive, plus you met Sharon. That makes it better, does it not?"

Gale was glad to see Daniel smile.

Daniel became serious and told Gale about the incident on the boat with the two thugs. "There is no doubt that they were intending to capture Sharon. How does that fit into your Heaven?"

"First of all, it's not my Heaven and second of all what happened to the two of you is a conundrum to me. For them to be able to capture someone from their reality they must be Guardians—Guardians gone bad unfortunately."

"That would make Heaven more like Earth than I would like," Daniel responded. \

"I agree," said Gale.

"Come in Guardians. Over." A crackly voice emanated from inside the tent.

Daniel found the two-way radio under a sleeping bag. "Hello Mr. Yamoto. Are you at the top? Over."

"Almost, I am at Hillary's Step. It's a pretty hard climb but unbelievably the ropes that were put here by Sherpas on Earth are here now. Once I go up it's only a matter of an easy 300 meter stroll to the summit. Over."

"Then get going and keep us informed. Most importantly be careful. Over." Gale doubted that anything on Everest could be consider a stroll. Yamoto had been climbing for hours and though this was Heaven, he was experiencing all of the same effects as if real. "Thank you and I mean thank you. Out." The radio went silent.

Gale felt good about the decision they had made to let Yamoto try again and he said so to Daniel. During his existence in Heaven, Gale had never had cause for or even an inclination to question "God's Plan." His existence—especially after joining up with his beloved Elizabeth—had been perfect. He would have been content just staying with his family in the *home existence* they were living in. But he also felt good about the work he was doing as a Guardian. In many cases he was able to set the culprit straight and put them in a situation where they could enjoy their afterlife. Of course the deportations were exceptionally disturbing, but he never had any qualms that the person was deserving of their punishment. Maybe for a person of the 21st century, such as Daniel, Heaven might be a disappointment. For a person such as himself who lived in the early 19th century, Heaven was just that, heaven.

Gale still had strong memories of his life on Earth. Much was good—home and hearth and such. Of course there was much that wasn't so good. He never realized how bad the odors were in his life until he died—there was no stench in Heaven. There was also no death in Heaven, at least not like it was on Earth. Gale remembered that death was a constant part of life. Everyday someone Gale knew or knew of died. Infants died by the drove. Disease claimed so many of all ages, and mysterious epidemics could wipe out whole neighborhoods. Daniel could never realize how big a part death played in Gale's time. He lived in an advanced society with medicines that pretty much eliminated the great killers of Gale's time. Cholera, typhoid, plagues—the list seemed endless and just thinking of these menaces made Gale shudder.

Gale's contemplation was interrupted by Daniel speaking, "Come in Yamoto. Can you give us an update? Over."

No response.

"Yamoto. Do you copy? Over."

Silence.

Daniel dropped the radio in frustration. "I have a feeling he got hurt somehow. Can we go get him?"

"Of course we can and if he is hurt we can think him directly to Central." Gale thought about how cold he had been when they had arrived. "Though I suggest we take a moment to make sure we are as warmly dressed as possible."

Daniel laughed. "I thought you were turning into a frozen Popsicle before. I don't think I've ever seen anyone look as cold as you did."

Gale wasn't sure what a Popsicle was but he knew what frozen meant. "I don't think anyone ever felt as cold as I felt."

Their quick search of the tent netted them a pair of quality gloves and a parka for Gale and sun-blocking goggles for both. They were not as well prepared for the mountain as they should be but they were not planning a trek. They just had to get Yamoto and go.

"As soon as we get to him, Daniel, check to make sure he has not expired—again."

With that Gale said, "Let's go." The familiar shimmering began and the relative comfort of the tent began to fade away.

With their first arrival on Everest the two Guardians had been blasted by wind and cold of almost incomprehensible magnitude. Now, just as with the first appearance, Daniel gasped. But this time it was not a gasp caused by the wind or cold but from the sunshine and incredible grandeur of the scene around him.

Forgetting for an instant about Yamoto, Daniel turned a complete circle and except for a small ridge of snow that inclined slightly upward, all that he saw was below him. In the distance he saw mountains peaks—probably giant in their own right—which looked like small hills from his vantage point. He was at the top of the world, albeit not the real world as on Earth, but he was still experiencing something he could never have hoped to experience in life. Daniel hated thinking that only the experiences on Earth were real—the implication being that this was somehow not real. Though vastly different, existence in Heaven was as real as life on Earth. His feelings for Sharon were real, his anger and fear over the boat incident were real. The euphoria he felt at this instant was real, as was the cold and the wind and the danger.

This feeling of well-being was suddenly crushed when he heard Gale shout, "Where is Yamoto?" The two men seemed to be alone on the ridge. The snow was deep but not deep enough to cover a man's body. Looking down Daniel saw a bright red rope coming out of the snow and disappearing over the edge. After pointing the rope out to Gale, Daniel knelt down and carefully peered over the side. He became less tentative when he felt Gale grasp his shoulder for added security.

About ten feet below them Daniel saw the inert body of Yamoto. He was attached to the rope by a single hook. His body was bent backward and he was swinging slightly in the breeze. His eyes were closed and he was either unconscious or dead. "I think we should pull him up and then decide what action to take." Gale said looking over Daniel's shoulder.

Hoping that the bottom of the rope wasn't firmly attached, the Guardians cleared away the snow and both took hold. "Ready, pull." They shouted in unison. Pulling with all of their strength, heels digging into the snow, the rope moved. Reestablishing secure footholds they pulled again and again the rope moved. Slowly and with exceptional effort they got Yamoto to the edge. "Hang on," Daniel shouted to Gale. "I'll grab him."

"Go ahead," came the breathless response.

Letting go of his hold on the rope, Daniel dived forward. He could see Yamoto start to slip downward. He desperately thrust his arms over the edge. He grasped Yamoto's parka like a lioness holding her cub by the scruff—but realized he was sliding inexorably towards the edge. He knew he had just moments before he was dragged over. If he let Yamoto go the fall would probably break his back. If he didn't Daniel knew that he would be pulled over and be killed. In the instant after his mind told his hand to let go and before his hands opened up Daniel felt a strong grip on his ankles.

"I got you Danny-boy, now hold on."

Between Gale's powerful legs and Daniel's arm strength they pulled Yamoto's torso over the edge. One more tug and his whole bottom lay on top. Feeling as if was drowning Daniel gasped for breath in the thin air. The exertion of his hard breathing seemed to use more air than he could bring in. He forgot his own struggles when he looked at Yamoto and saw his eyes were open. He was obviously dazed but he was breathing and seemed okay.

With wordless agreement, Daniel and Gale struggled to their feet. Laboriously they slowly pulled Yamoto to his feet. But rather than heading directly to Central Booking, they turned toward the summit of the great mountain and took a step, then another. Like a six-legged monster, with two feet out of order, they stumbled and dragged, rested, stumbled and dragged, rested. The pain in his lungs was excruciating. He had to suck in so hard just to get any air at all, that Daniel felt as if his ribs were cracking in his chest with each breath he took.

Yamoto had said the summit was only 200 meters from the Hillary step. That was roughly 600 feet, Daniel calculated. Each of their pathetic steps seemed about six inches—1/2 of a foot. That meant 1,200 steps—at their current pitiful rate of progress Daniel calculated it would take them six years to get to the summit. He smiled at his oxygen deprived joke. Looking at Gale he was thankful—thankful to God seemed appropriate—that he was his partner. William Gale was, Daniel believed, one of those rare people who were truly good. Good to his family, good to his friends, good to his fellow man—just good. Not great, good. *That's probably better*, Daniel thought. Greatness always seemed to come with a countervailing badness or character flaw. As of yet Daniel hadn't found any character flaws in William—just goodness.

In the distance Daniel could see some small flags fluttering in the wind. They were sticking from a snow cornice that Daniel knew was the summit. As they approached Daniel saw that William was smiling. He also felt Yamoto stirring.

"Mr. Yamoto, Mr. Yamoto," he heard Gale shout. "You've made it. We are approaching the peak."

With those words, Yamato looked up and a new found strength seemed to envelope his whole being. His Holy Grail was a few moments away. A lifetime of failed attempts that had ultimately led to his death were about to be erased. He stood up on his own accord. He looked a Daniel then at William. A great smiled appeared, while at the same time tears welled up in his eyes. The Guardians released their helping holds and he proudly straightened his back and began to walk.

Time didn't seem to exist as the three new found friends reached the top of their old world. No words were spoken, none were needed. Daniel watched as Yamoto pushed the small Japanese flag into the snow, he then reached inside his parka and took out a beautiful golden frame that held a black and white picture. With great reverence and affection Yamoto placed the picture of his father on the top of Mt. Everest. He bowed his head for a moment then stood and looking at the Guardians he again bowed his head and said, "Thank you."

Daniel and William reached out touched his shoulder and this awe inspiring scene slowly began to shimmer and fade away.

Chapter 10

Unlike the drudgery of police work on Earth, Daniel was now sure that being a Guardian in Heaven was going to offer a dramatic variety of places and times. Having already been to Barbados, Woodstock, Mt. Everest, and the fringes of Hell, Daniel was not surprised to find Gale and himself in Paris. He had been to Paris with his ex-wife in what were a vastly different time and a completely different life. Looking around he realized that this Paris was also different than the one he had visited.

He could see the River Seine, but many of the bridges crossing it were constructed of wood. The roads were dirt, and there was no Eiffel Tower. Of course he already knew that they were after Legor Bedeau, a former Royal Guard who was skulking around Paris during Bastille Day—the original Bastille Day. He was on the prowl for vulnerable women and when he found one he sexually attacked her. Obviously Bedeau's lust for perverse satisfaction was overruling any sense of morality he might have—which, for all Daniel knew may have been zero. Daniel felt that he was seeing that the human desire for over-indulgence was as prevalent in Heaven as it had been on Earth.

"I guess it's not that different here than on Earth." Daniel voiced the thought that had been in his mind for some time. "Temptation can cause good people to do bad things and bad people to do horrendous things." He thought about the cases he knew of during his life when cops had turned. He remembers times when he was tempted, usually when sexual favors were offered. Daniel had done his best to avoid the temptations available to almost all cops—he had not always been successful. The sexual transgressions were a major factor in the breakup of his marriage.

He knew what tempted policemen on Earth, but what would make a Guardian risk eternal damnation? Some of the causes were probably not the same since money was a non-factor here. Of course power and perverse sexual satisfaction were probably the prevalent causes as they were on Earth.

"What would make a Guardian risk hell?" He asked Gale. "Especially considering that we, more than most, really know what Hell is all about."

"I truly don't know, Danny-boy. This is the first time I've come across it. But I do know that we are about to find out." Paris, circa 1789, passed by as the two men talked about their assignment.

Gale continued, "Because Bedeau was a Guardian we should err on the cautious side and assume that he still has all of the powers we have. This will make his capture more difficult and more dangerous than usual..."

"More dangerous than a Nazi Concentration camp or the top of Mt Everest?"

Ignoring Daniel's sarcasm Gale continued, "Now, most of these people are here to celebrate the storming of the fortress that basically began the French Revolution—not much after your own revolution. And unless we run into Louis XIV himself, most of the people should be festive and gay."

Gale's assertion was proven true by the friendly nods and greetings they received from others. Almost all of the women were dressed in bright colored dresses that were, Daniel assumed, the style of the time. They carried matching parasols to protect them from the noonday sun, which they casually spun on their shoulders.

While Daniel took in the scenery Gale explained some of the basics of Paris life during this time period. "Conditions in France were pretty bad. There had been a drought that led to crop failures and then to food shortages. King Louis XVI needed money so he convened the Estates General in order to levy a new land tax that would hopefully solve his monetary woes. Unfortunately for the King, the part of the Estates General that represented the people took charge. Louis then tried to shut it down but the members resisted and instead of raising new taxes they decided to write a new constitution."

"Like our Continental Congress," Daniel said.

"Well that was a meeting of revolutionaries," Gale responded. He smiled and added, "Who were traitors against a just king. Louis, on the other hand, was somewhat of a despot."

Though Gale seemed to be well versed in the causes of the French Revolution Daniel was more concerned with the here and now. "That's all well and good but I don't think a history lesson will help us catch Bedeau." He regretted saying anything the second he saw the hurt look on Gale's face. "Sorry William, I just have a bad feeling about this assignment."

"No need to apologize Danny-boy, as my Elizabeth says 'William, my dear husband, you will need all of eternity and then some to say all of the things you want to say'."

Daniel stopped abruptly when a shop window caught his attention. Glistening in the sunlight he saw a beautiful gold sword and gem encrusted scabbard.

"You know I would have kept walking and talking if I hadn't noticed that you had disappeared."

"Oh I'm sorry about that, but look." Daniel pointed to the sword.

"That is a very nice foil indeed," Gale said as he walked up to the glass for a better look. "The hilt looks to be very well made. I like the taper and width, very important to effective thrust."

Daniel stood with his mouth slightly open as Gale spoke. As an eighth level black belt in Karate, Daniel was well trained in sword play, but here in front of him was a man for whom swords were a part of everyday life—as television and computers were for Daniel. "Are we allowed to arm ourselves?" Daniel asked.

"I don't see why not," Gale replied. He tried the door and it opened.

The store was dark with the only source of light being the front window. "Hello. Anyone here?" Daniel called out. No answer was forthcoming and Daniel assumed the store was empty. He walked to the window display and picked up the sword. "So what's the deal, can we take this sword or would that be stealing?"

"Well since it does not belong to us I think it would be stealing," Gale responded.

"And since it belongs to me I would agree," the strange voice came from a dark corner of the room. The speaker walked into the light. He was a heavyset man with long white hair and was, Daniel guessed, dressed as a shopkeeper from 18th century would be dressed. A dour Mr. Fezziwig popped into his mind as his only frame of reference.

"I'm sorry," said Daniel, "I should have known better. My name is Daniel Lambert, my friend here is William Gale and we are Guardians on assignment to this time and place." He thought about reaching out to shake hands but because he was woefully ignorant of different customs and didn't want to offend the man, he decided to just smile politely.

"I've met one of your kind before; he was a former King's Guard and a vulgar bully if I ever met one." The man showed his disgust by mimicking spitting on the floor.

Gale and Daniel looked at each other with excitement. "Did you meet him recently?" Gale got the words out first.

Ignoring Gale's question the man closely looked over the two Guardians. He seemed to be especially interested in Gale's impressive uniform and much less so in Daniel's very unofficial non-descript slacks and jacket. "When and where are you gentlemen from?"

That was the first time Daniel heard *when* included with *where* in that context and it certainly made the question more germane. "I am from 21st century United States and Mr. Gale is from 19th century London." This time Daniel beat Gale to the punch. "I gather this is your time and place."

"You would gather correctly then, Mister." Though Daniel heard Mister he knew the shopkeeper had said Monsieur. The Heavenly translator was very literal and did not take into account different idioms and slang terms. Looking at Daniel he said, "I am somewhat surprised you country survived so many years. I always believed that too much freedom for the masses was not a good thing."

"By the time I died, we were losing freedoms faster than a drunk loses brain cells," Daniel said without thinking. He really wanted to focus on the matter at hand and besides, Earthly politics being about as moot as could be in this existence, Daniel pressed the man on his meeting with the ex-Guardian. Unfortunately the shopkeeper had his own agenda and his conversation wandered from his heavenly travels to the people he had met in his shop. It was Gale who tried to take charge of the situation by changing the subject.

"I really like this Claymore," he said as he hefted a massive double-edged sword. "I believe this sword was used by Scottish Highlanders against the crown in the 16th Century."

The portly man looked at Gale with newfound respect. "You British know your swords, though your sword-play was never as refined as we French?"

"Can we get back to the subject at hand?" Daniel's impatience was evident as he fidgeted nervously. His police sense was in high alert and he was about to express his concern to Gale when the back door burst open. Instinct took over and being from a time of gangs and guns, Daniel immediately hit the deck. Gale, on the other hand came from a different time, rather than duck he stood tall, picked up the giant Claymore sword in both hands, and prepared for a fight. Daniel, inspired by Gale's steadfastness, grabbed the foil that he had seen in the window and stood by Gale—his partner and his friend—who nodded and gave him a sly smile.

Three men faced Gale and Daniel in the fading light of the now very crowded shop. They recognized one as Bedeau. He was impeccably dressed in the garish and imposing uniform of the King's Guard. Bedeau and his two lieutenants had their swords drawn and slowly moved towards the Guardians.

In a calm but grandiloquent manner Bedeau said, "You may run now if you choose. We will not stop you. It may be dishonorable but at least you won't have to die…again."

Before Daniel could tell Bedeau to go fuck himself, Gale said, "Actually I would suggest that you surrender like a good gentleman." He was looking intently at Bedeau. "Your friends may leave the way they came." To Daniel he said under his breath, "You deal with the lackeys I'll take care of Bedeau."

In the next instant Gale saw a slender blade lunging towards his chest. Beating it aside he struck with all of the speed and strength he could muster. He could see the man's eyes widen in horror as Daniel's sword plunged through his neck severing arteries and veins as it made its voyage of death.

Without hesitation and without compassion Daniel wrenched the blade free before the man fell. With blood splattering everywhere and madness enveloping him Daniel could see a cutlass blade slicing through the skin of his arm and felt a numbing shock as it struck bone. Ignoring the agony he threw his injured arm up over his head taking the cutlass with it. His assailants' chest then became an unprotected target that Daniel easily found with his sword.

With his quarries dispatched Daniel turned toward Gale and Bedeau who were embroiled in a battle of incredible skill and dexterity. The expertise of the two men was evident in each thrust and parry and Daniel watched with fascination. The dreamlike feeling of being a dissociated spectator was being fueled by his loss of blood. *I've got to either abandon William and head back to Central or stop the blood loss*, he thought. Without any hesitation he ripped off his jacket and wrapped it around his wounded arm. The wound was way too deep for the blood to be stopped by this makeshift tourniquet and Daniel knew he was risking Heaven-death by not returning to Central. Of course he also knew he would never leave Gale. Though he could hear the metallic clang as sword met sword, his vision was fading quickly and he was about to lose consciousness. *Where should I go*, he thought, *Cen...*

"Daniel. Daniel. Can you hear me?"

The bright light hurt his eyes as he woke. Staring at him was the familiar and very concerned face of Gale.

Chapter 11

"Daniel. Daniel. Can you hear me?"

The bright light hurt his eyes as he woke. Staring at him was the familiar and very concerned face of William Gale. "We are back in the nest, safe and sound," Gale said. "You were badly hurt but it looks like you'll be fine."

"Did you get Bedeau?"

"No he slipped out when you fell. By the way Danny-boy you seemed quite capable with that sword—for a modern man that is."

Daniel thought about the fight and his foes. "Are those men dead? I mean Heaven-dead. I mean did I kill them?"

"Yes, Daniel, they are Heaven-dead as you say. Of course, death in Heaven is as much a mystery as it was on Earth."

"Would their bodies be there if we went back right now?" Daniel asked.

"No, they would be gone and please don't ask me where they go—I haven't the foggiest idea."

Daniel realized that this led credence to the idea that one's body in Heaveneaven was the ethereal part of ones existence—a vessel for the soul. This was the polar opposite to life on Earth where the body was real and the soul was intangible.

"What about Bedeau? Do we go after him or just wait for our next assignment?"

Gale smiled. "You seem to have quite a few questions. It reminds me of when my children were young; 'Father, why does it rain? Why is the sky blue?'"

Daniel looked down sheepishly. "I'm sorry but sometimes I feel like the proverbial *Babe in the Woods*."

Gale patted Daniel on the shoulder. "I meant no harm, Danny-boy. I loved it when my son asked questions and I feel the same with you. I'm just sorry that I don't have all of the answers."

Daniel shook his head with incredulity. But before he could speak information came into his head that Bedeau was now in a 16th century castle somewhere in the Carpathian Mountains.

"There's one of your answers, Danny-boy."

"Let's go get this ass-hole," Daniel said. Gale smiled as they began to dematerialize.

The pair reappeared at the base of a massive stone wall that extended so far up that the men could not see the top. "There is a reason that we appeared here rather than inside," Gale said in a hushed voice. "The powers, or power, that be, must anticipate that Bedeau will have accomplices ready to fight for him."

"I guess a stealthy entrance is needed," Daniel responded as they began walking along the base of the wall. As they walked Daniel saw two heavy sticks. Picking them up he handed one to Gale. "They may not be as good as the swords we had in France but they are certainly better than nothing."

Gale took the stick hitting his palm as if to test its strength. "This could prove useful, Thank you. You know Daniel, just because I have never come across organized crime societies or gangs in Heaven does not mean they don't exist. Two people with the same deviant predilections might meet by chance. They could then recruit others and before you can say Bessarabians you have a society of blaggards. Unfortunately we Guardians are unprepared to deal with an organized group."

"William, I've been thinking the same thing. I'm also a little concerned that we have no way of knowing if there are one, two or a hundred bad guys in this castle." Daniel said as they began walking again.

Gale laughed and Daniel looked at him quizzically.

"I meant we as a police force are not set up to deal with organized groups," Gale said. "Of course you are correct in you assessment of the situation."

As they walked Daniel's thoughts began to drift towards Sharon. He wondered what she was doing right now. Of course *right now* had no relevance in Heaven where different realities were not concurrent in time or space. Even the passage of time meant nothing when compared to another reality. Only when he and Sharon were together—which he wished was right now—did their individual existences synchronize with each other.

Daniel's happy contemplation was interrupted when he walked right into Gale. "Daydreaming about a lady, Danny-boy?"

"Not me," Daniel responded sheepishly. "I'm as ready as a cat…"

"A cat-napper, maybe."

Both men were smiling and despite the unknown situation they were about to face, were content, almost happy, as they continued walking. They had become an effective pair and Daniel realized that Gale was as good a partner as he had ever had. He also realized that they were now friends.

"Finally a way in," Gale said as he stopped in front of an archway cut into the wall. As they walked through what they hoped was an entryway the true scale of the fortress became evident from the thickness of the wall.

"This place was built to last," Daniel observed. "But this

doorway seems like an Achilles heel. I'm surprised it's not guarded."

"During its Earthly existence I am sure there would have been a sentry detail. But in Heaven it does not matter. People can corporealize anywhere."

"I guess that's why it was *decided* that we walk in."

The light coming into the tunnel was decreasing as they walked, but before it disappeared altogether the walkway ended in a small chamber encircled by a stone stairway.

"Upwards and onwards," Gale proclaimed as the climbed the stairs.

The stairway was well lit from above and as they neared the top they heard muffled voices and stopped. "I don't think we are prepared for an assault on this castle," Daniel whispered.

"Well since we forgot our siege train," Gale said referring to the age old method of attacking stone fortresses, "our actions will have to be ad libitum."

"Ad libitum or not I'm swinging first and asking questions later," Daniel said raising his ersatz club.

Gale smiled at his impetuous partner. "I don't think we have to make a Light Brigade charge. We have no idea how many are inside or if they will protect Bedeau."

"So, we walk in like we own the place and ask for Bedeau," Daniel said facetiously.

Gale laughed, "No, we walk in, try to blend in, and find Bedeau on our own."

"Sounds like a plan," Daniel said keeping his club at the ready, "a pretty crappy one, but it is a plan."

The stairway ended on a landing that opened into a large open air courtyard. The people's whose voices they had heard were no where to be seen. The sides of the courtyard were lined with doors and windows and Daniel grabbed the handle of the first door they came to. It was unlocked and as their eyes adjusted to the darkness inside they could see they were in a candlelit foyer. The walls were decorated with paintings of long dead, but possibly still here, noblemen and women, as well as beautiful tapestries depicting battles and hunting parties.

Both men stopped at the same time when the heard voices coming from a closed door. "Why are you doing this to me," said a very frightened woman's voice.

"Shut up you whore, or I'll shut you up," responded an angry male voice. They then heard the sound of a slap followed by sobbing.

Instinctively Daniel reached for the door handle.

Grabbing his hand before he could open the door, Gale said, "No Daniel, that is not Bedeau and he, and only he, is our assignment."

"But that woman is in trouble, and we have to help her."

"We have a job to do and we have to do it." Gale responded sternly. Looking across the hall he pointed to another door, "Bedeau is there."

"How the hell do you…" Daniel started to say. But before finishing the sentence the realization that Bedeau was in there came in to his mind as well. *What a place*, Daniel thought.

With reluctance Daniel followed Gale to the doorway. Grabbing the handle Gale whispered, "One…two…three…Open!" Pushing the latch he thrust open the, luckily, unlocked door.

Bursting into the room they saw Bedeau standing at a window looking out. Determined to get to him before he could disappear, Gale and Daniel sprinted across the room. Bedeau turned shouting "Bastards!" and rather than trying to escape he pulled his sword.

Daniel reached Bedeau first and swung his stick directly at

Bedeau's sword hand. Connecting hard Daniel heard Bedeau gasp in pain and saw his sword drop to the floor. At that same moment Gale hit Bedeau on the head with his stick. Daniel heard the thud at watched as Bedeau collapsed to the floor.

"I was not going to give that crafty bastard a chance to escape."

Daniel was a little surprised by the hint of blood lust in Gale's voice. "Well, let's get him to Central a sap," Daniel said. As he said this he hesitated slightly, allowing Gale to reach for Bandeaux's shoulder. Gale looked at Daniel who now had a sly smile. "No, Daniel..." Gale said but it was too late for he and Bedeau shimmered then disappeared before he could finish his pleading.

Without any hesitation Daniel ran straight for the door where they had heard the woman in trouble. "Here I go again," Daniel said to himself as he pushed the door open. The scene that confronted him made him pause. A stark naked man stood in the middle of the room. Below him and clearly being menaced by him lay a naked woman crying. A leather strap bound the two wrist to wrist. Though he had more pressing issues at that moment, the thought came to Daniel that the strap linked the woman to man and prohibited her from disappearing. It was also exactly like the strap that the thugs had tried to use on Sharon. Realizing that he had to move fast, Daniel took a page from Gale's playbook and without hesitating clunked the man on the head.

"Are you okay," Daniel asked as he averted his eyes from the woman.

"You can look, and yes I'm fine," she responded. Daniel glanced and saw the woman was standing now and fully dressed in jeans and a t-shirt.

"I couldn't do anything when that leather strap attached me to this...man."

So the strap must give the wielder the same imprisoning power that guardians have, and that's a little disconcerting, Daniel thought. Gale had never mentioned a tool such as this and he wondered if they were common things in Heaven. It reminded Daniel of the crime wars, all wars for that matter, on Earth. One side developed speed radar, the other developed radar detectors; one developed bulletproof vests the other body armor piercing bullets; and so on forever. It seemed that Heaven was the same as Earth, endless escalation in the name of gaining an edge or power over someone else. Turning his attention to the woman, he hoped to get some more information from her.

"Why did this man capture you?" Daniel realized he knew the answer, and not wanting to embarrass the poor woman he quickly added, "I mean you in particular."

"I have no idea. I haven't been dead very long and was existing with my grandparents in Vermont around 1955." She explained using the vernacular of place and time that Daniel was finding common in Heaven. "This man just appeared, grabbed me and took me away. I couldn't do anything when he got that strap around my arm. I tried to get away, you know, think myself away, but that strapped wouldn't let me. I wanted to kill myself but I'm already dead." She started to sob but stopped abruptly. "There are more of these shitheads around, I could hear them. So please understand that I have no intention of sticking around."

"But I want to ask a few questions," Daniel implored. But it was too late, she was already shimmering and beginning to disappear. Before she was gone Daniel saw her mouth the words, "Thank you."

Hearing some commotion in the hallway Daniel thought about investigating further but his common sense told him that would not be a good idea, and might be a dangerous course to take. He decided discretion was the better part of valor so, *Central Booking,* he thought.

"Tsk, tsk, tsk," Gale said as Daniel appeared. Standing next to him was Mr. Lee, looking as stoic as ever.

"Where's Bedeau? That woman we heard had been captured. I freed her but she left before I could ask her any questions. We need to find out what's going on at that castle."

"Always the good police officer," Gale said. "But we are not really police officers anymore. We are Guardians and we just do our assignments."

"Don't start with that crap now. Where's Bedeau?"

"I am sorry, Mr. Lambert," Said Mr. Lee. "I have sent Mr. Bedeau on to his eternal damnation."

"Fuck," Daniel said forgetting his pledge.

"Just stop thinking about it, Daniel," Gale said. "There really is not anything we can do, except our jobs."

"Tell that to the woman raped by that asshole," Daniel spit out the words, "or the others who might be held in that castle. With God-knows-what being done to them." *If God knows anything,* Daniel thought.

Trying to console him, Gale put his hand on Daniel's shoulder. Not wanting to be consoled, Daniel angrily pushed it off.

Regretting the move Daniel said, "I'm sorry William but I've been trained to help people. And I can't believe you wouldn't help someone in need."

"I would like to think that we are helping. This is our after-life also and we could just enjoy it without the responsibility and risk that comes with being a Guardian.

Not wanting to argue anymore Daniel just shook his head.

"And I'm sure God will deal with the miscreants at the proper time."

"Fine," was Daniel's response, though he was a little surprised to hear a small hint of doubt about God from William.

"Why don't you go visit Mrs. Sharon. I am sure she will help get your mind straight," Gale said with a wink.

"Look, William, I like you but…"

"Just go Danny-Boy, just go," William said just before disappearing.

Chapter 12

Before he was even fully materialized Daniel felt someone jump into his arms and begin kissing his face. "I hope this is Sharon," he said before finding her lips and kissing back.

Although she felt very light in his arms and he would have gladly kept her there for as long as he could he set her down and stepped back. "You are a sight for sore eyes Sharon, a sight for sore eyes."

"Bad day at the office, Mr. Lambert?" she responded with a smile.

"Day, week, year, I'm not sure how long but yes it was a little disconcerting. I'm finding out things about Heaven that have me a little concerned. When William and…" In mid sentence Sharon put her finger on his lips.

"Not now Daniel, you and I are alone together. This is now our existence. Well not completely alone," Sharon said looking down.

Looking down Daniel could see and feel a smallish black cat rubbing against his pants. "I'll be damned, a cat!"

"This is Puma, my friend from my life." She said as she bent down and picked up the cat. "This is Daniel," she said in the cat's ears.

"So all dogs do go to Heaven," Daniel said reaching out to scratch the felines head.

"Not a dog, Daniel, she is a cat."

"I know, I was just referring to a movie that came out long after you had passed on. I didn't realize that our pets joined us here. The fact that they do should erase the lies of millions of parents who explained the death of a gerbil, fish or any other pet to their children. Saying Fido is in doggy heaven wasn't quite correct; Fido is in people heaven."

"I remember my Aunt telling me that my pet rabbit was in rabbit heaven when it got hit by a car. I must have been nine or ten. Though my Uncle wasn't too happy with my Aunt for trying to comfort me—he was pretty orthodox—it made me feel better believing her so I did." She smiled at the memory.

"So she was here when you got here or did she appear later?" Daniel asked.

"She was here as part of this reality," Sharon responded as she swung her arms to point out her home. "I can't bring her with me when I travel. I've tried by holding her tightly as I transport to another reality but she doesn't travel with me. It is a little strange considering my clothes do transport."

As did the note she gave him when they first met, Daniel recalled.

"Of course she is always here waiting when I return, and she is none the worse for wear."

"Do you have to feed her?" Daniel asked.

"Not unless I want to and if I don't feed her there is no litter box to clean."

Sharon seemed happy having her beloved pet with her but Daniel wondered if she ever questioned the cat's authenticity. Seeing her stroke the cat's fur he realized that the affection between the two was real—whether Puma was or not—and what better place than Heaven for true feelings to be realized. He knew that the emotions that he was developing for Sharon were as real as anything he had felt in life.

"Just another completely baffling aspect of heaven," Daniel said as Sharon set Puma down. The cat immediately jumped onto a window perch which looked out over a large river.

"What a view," Daniel exclaimed as he and Sharon walked, hand in hand, to the window. Seeing a sailboat Daniel picked up a pair of binoculars that Sharon kept on the sill. It was an older boat and Daniel could easily make out the two men sitting in the boat's cockpit. The boat was well trimmed and Daniel surmised that they knew what they were doing.

He wondered if they could use their binoculars and see him. "I see that boat quite often." Sharon said. "Sometimes they even wave to me."

Daniel put down the binoculars and gave a quick pat on the head to Puma. "These are the little things about Heaven that keep me wondering. How is it that of all of the infinite *times* that existed for this place they happen to be in the exact same one as us."

"And why them?" Sharon asked, continuing Daniel's though process. "There must have been tens of thousands of people who lived and died her, including me and those two men. Yet there are not tens of thousands of people milling about. This house was over seventy years old when I bought it so where are the previous owners?"

"My partner always says to just accept things," Daniel said. "And he seems happy and he certainly has been here much longer than I have. But I think I can do a better job if I knew more on how things worked in this place."

"And as for you young lady," Daniel said putting his arms around Sharon. "How could you have lived in this beautiful place, with so much water around you, and not be a first-class sailor?"

"I do agree it's beautiful but let me show you where I spent most of my life." Grabbing his hand again, Sharon led Daniel to a door which she opened taking them outside into a beautiful day.

The academia atmosphere was obvious. Large trees lined the streets and the buildings were brick and covered in ivy

"This is where I spent most of my time, Dalhousie University. As a matter of fact this is where I still spend most of my time. Heaven is a wonderful place, Daniel. I know it is very confusing but one can be very happy here."

Realizing how true her words were, Daniel couldn't help saying, "I know. I was never this happy in life." He regretted letting his feelings out like that but felt much better when Sharon smiled at him.

"Me too," Sharon said softly.

"So you were a professor here. I bet the boys signed up for your classes just to be in your class, they probably didn't even care what the subject was."

Over the next few hours Daniel and Sharon walked the campus. She showed him her office and in her lecture hall Daniel sat in the first row while Sharon gave him a quick lesson in Societal Anthropology. Her zeal and love for the topic made him love it also. And though he was clueless as to the subject matter, he didn't even have to feign interest, though he did begin to focus more on her than her words. She was definitely a beautiful woman, and though her life (at least the early part of it) was filled with sadness and tragedy, Daniel saw a spark in her that told him she was happy and had no regrets towards her life or with her death.

"Mr. Lambert, are you paying attention?" The words roused Daniel from his inattentiveness.

"Yes ma'am," he replied with exaggerated remorseful.

"Okay, let's see," Sharon responded continuing the charade. "Who was the social anthropologist who wrote extensively on girls' initiation rites?"

"Let me see," Daniel said pensively. "Girls' initiation rites..." Sharon must have said the name but Daniel didn't have the foggiest idea.

As he walked on to the stage he pretended to mull over the question. He walked to Sharon and put his arms around her. "Did this person consider hugging an initiation rite?" He asked as he put his arms around her.

"Yes she did."

"How about kissing?" He asked as he brought his mouth to Sharon's.

"Hmm uh," She mumbled as their lips met.

"How about making love?" He whispered in her ear.

"That was one of the most important." She answered as they began to unbutton each other's shirts.

Every day that he spent with Sharon, Daniel had to remind himself that he was dead. It all seemed so normal. They spent their time as one would expect of a couple in love; long nights (and sometimes days) of love-making, picnics on the bluffs overlooking the harbor, strolls through downtown Halifax.

Even the city seemed normal. Cafes had customers—they were not as busy as on Earth, according to Sharon—but the patrons they did have were drinking coffee and socializing. In the cafe they visited there was even a young woman working the espresso machine and like the bartender in Barbados who decided working in a bar was his heavenly reward, this young lady—Rachel was her name—had decided that being a barista was her idea of heaven. Daniel made no judgment on their choices, especially considering he was—as he was on Earth—a policeman in heaven.

There was a sense of time passing. Each day turned into night and then day again. The weather varied as it did on Earth. It was chilly in the morning, pleasantly warm under the sunshine and cold at night. But the other indicators of time were absent. Daniel never became hungry or tired, yet they ate and slept. Daniel found Sharon to be an excellent cook, a gourment when compared to Daniel's experiences, and he looked forward to the surprise dishes she served him.

When he exerted himself he got sweaty and took a shower. He brushed his teeth and shaved. He noticed that Puma did the things one would expect a cat to do, she played and groomed, she slept, a lot Daniel noticed, and in general acted as a cat would on Earth.

It was all so normal but it was also very surreal. It was truly living in the moment. He was very glad for those moments he was living in, especially since he was sharing them with Sharon.

"Do season change?" he asked her one morning as they walked along one of the many walking paths near her home. "I mean, if we stayed put in your house for 120 sunrises and sunsets would it become winter?"

She chuckled then said, "Believe it or not, I did just that. I sat and read over sixty novels without leaving the house. I didn't keep track of the days but it was easily three months worth."

"I would have gone nuts just sitting around for three months," Daniel responded.

"As much as I love reading, I don't think I could have read for that long when I was alive without going a little stir crazy," she said. "But it was strange, I had no sense of time passing, either passing quickly or dragging slowly."

"I guess that's how it has to be if one is to spend an eternity existing here especially here," he said jokingly.

"You heel and need I remind you that I loved playing rugby and was quite good," she said as she tackled him. They landed in a heap on the soft grass unscathed and laughing.

"How quaint." The words broke their reverie and as Sharon

rolled off of him Daniel saw a man standing over them. The sun shone brightly behind him so Daniel could not make out his features.

"May I help you?" Daniel asked as he subtly pushed Sharon behind him and prepared himself for whatever might come next. After the insident on the boat Daniel was taking no more chances.

"Oh no and please excuse me for the interruption." Daniel relaxed slightly as he realized that the stranger seemed to be of no threat. "Sharon…Sharon Jaffee, is that you?" He said with obvious excitement.

"Oh my God," Sharon screamed. "Professor Templeton." She quickly got up and ran to the man and gave him a hug of genuine affection."

"I would normally say 'it's a small world' but this isn't a world and I have no idea how big or small it is anyway," Daniel said as he stood, dusted himself off, and offered his hand to the man.

"Professor Templeton this is my friend Daniel Lambert." Sharon introduced the two as they shook hands. "The professor was a dear friend of mine at Dalhousie." She said to Daniel. "He really helped me navigate the treacherous waters of Academia."

"Sharon was a breath of fresh air," The Professor said with genuine affection, "and I just wanted to ensure her foray into that mostly men's club was, if not easy, at least not agonizingly difficult."

Daniel listened as the two discussed the old days at Dalhousie. There relationship had obviously been like that of a close father and daughter. When Daniel expressed his surprise that the two hadn't met up before, Professor Templeton explained his theory as to why that was so.

"Place is easy in Heaven. I have not adapted well to calling this place Heaven. To me it's more like Second Life."

"Or Second Chance from what I've seen since arriving," Daniel said.

"Daniel is a Guardian," Sharon interjected.

"Ah, a constable of Civitas Dei. I would be safe in assuming that you never expected your eternal rest would be eternal vigilance."

Daniel smiled at the Professor's words though he wasn't 100% sure that he understood every one of them.

"You were saying, Professor," Sharon chimed in.

"Yes I was saying. What was saying, Sharon dear?

"You were explaining your ideas on meeting in Heaven…or should I say Second Life."

"I actually think it's quite simple. We, the denizens of Second Life have complete control over place but limited control over time. Though we gain more control over time when we are meeting a specific person. Now that I have met up with you, "he said to Sharon, "I can meet with you, and vice versa, whenever it is so desired. Time becomes a specific aspect of place."

"Sir Isaac had some similar theory's," Sharon said.

Professor Templeton's eyes widened. "Sir Isaac?"

"Newton that is," Daniel chimed in. "You know the guy with the apple."

"We should go back to see Sir Isaac and Victoria," Sharon said to Daniel. Then turning to the professor she said, "You should come with us, Professor, I think you and Sir Isaac would have plenty to talk about."

"By the way, Professor, how long after me did you pass on?" Sharon asked.

Professor Templeton fidgeted uncomfortably and Daniel notice his complexion turn ashen and his countenance became very serious. "It was less than two years, Sharon my dear."

Sharon, sensing the Professor's discomfiture discussing his

own death changed the subject. "I can't imagine a large turn out for my funeral."

"Oh no, quite the contrary. Dean Richardson closed the campus and rather than sleeping in as students are wont to do, I would estimate over 500 turned out to show their respects."

"Wow," Sharon said with genuine surprise. "I could barely get them to attend my classes during final examinations. There must have been food served."

"Okay, this is getting a little dark," Daniel chimed in.

"Come on, Daniel," Sharon said. You can't tell me that you never wondered when you were alive what your funeral would be like, who would come, who would cry. Those sorts of things."

"Actually, being a cop I tried to avoid any thoughts about dying." Though he did begin to wonder who was at his funeral and what they had said about him.

As if sharing a common notion, Daniel and Sharon both turned toward the Professor. He looked like a man who just had the weight of the world dropped on his shoulder. "Professor," Sharon asked with concern, "is everything all right?"

"No Sharon, everything is not all right. For two years after you died I lived with a horrible guilt, and it didn't lessen any after I died."

"What guilt could you have possibly had?" Sharon asked.

"When we come to heaven we leave all of our earthly offenses behind," Daniel quickly added. "Maybe we carry some of our predilections with us but we arrive with a clean slate."

"I may have a clean slate Guardian Lambert, but I have a very guilty conscience." Sharon and Daniel both sensed that he was very close to opening up, so they said nothing. As they expected the professor continued in a very somber voice. "Sharon, oh my dear Sharon," he said looking directly at her. "I'm the person who killed you."

Sharon's eyes became as large as oranges but she didn't say a word. He continued, "Jonathan and I were fighting." He turned to Daniel, "He was my sixteen year old son and we fought constantly. I was at my wits end so I went to the Rathskellar for a pint. Unfortunately one pint turned to two then three…

Daniel knew exactly where this was going. Stories like this had existed as long as people had been drinking alcohol and using any conveyance other then their feet to get home. He had certainly seen more than his share of tragedy as the result of drunk driving.

"I thought I was doing fine. When I came to the corner of Juniper and College I just kept on going. By the time I saw your car it was too late."

He could not go on and broke down in tears. Sharon, with tears also rolling down her cheeks hugged her dear friend. "It's okay Professor," she said as she stroked his hair. "You were like a father to me and I would never have blamed you."

"Thank you for that Sharon, but I couldn't forgive myself. Two years to the the day after the accident I was beyond distraught and took a full bottle of the barbiturates I had been prescribed for insomnia."

"Oh my God, Professor, you had so much to offer your students. Why would you do something so rash?" Sharon was almost scolding him. "One of your most endearing traits was your deliberateness."

"I'm not sure," he responded. "But I felt as if I was in Hell after I had killed you, so figured I might as well go there for real."

Sharon actually smiled. "Well you didn't go to hell and I wish you would stop saying you killed. It was an accident, nothing more."

"But Sharon…"

"Enough, Professor," Sharon interrupted.

"I agree," Daniel chimed in. "Heaven is as you said before

Second Life. Besides, I would hate to visit you in my professional capacity."

Sharon and Templeton looked at him in surprise.

"Believe it or not melancholy or extreme sadness are one the no-nos here." Daniel wasn't sure how he knew that fact but he did. He smiled, "Of course I can't imagine it being more than a misdemeanor."

During the weeks that followed the Professor become a regular and enjoyable part of their existence.

Chapter 13

It was a beautiful evening and Sharon and Daniel were sitting on a dock at the Armdale Yacht Club with their bare feet dangling over the edge being gently caressed by the water. The small waves lapping against the boats combined with the warm, damp air on their faces made them somnolent and they were reflective in their thoughts.

"Daniel," Sharon asked, "why did you leave your wife?"

Daniel thought for a second. He had never really summed the whole thing up before. Even with his divorce lawyer he had said it was his fault and he wasn't going to fight any request his soon-to-be e-wife made. He wanted to be truthful to Sharon but without too much detail.

"There was no single reason," he responded. "We were just drifting apart. I was a real jerk. Unlike now," he added. "I was moody and non-communicative. All the bad things a good husband should never be."

"What makes you so sure that *unlike now* is correct?" Sharon asked smiling.

Grabbing her by her shoulders and feigning throwing her in, Daniel continued. "I do remember that our last fight—the proverbial final straw—was over a spilt glass of pineapple juice. I was sitting watching T.V. when Carrie knocked an open glass of juice out of the fridge. Deborah freaked, not at Carrie or anything, just freaked. So I told her, *if you didn't leave an open glass this wouldn't have happened.*"

"That was not very smart, Daniel."

"You are correct ma'am. She then focused all that pent up anger on me." *Where it had always actually been*, Daniel thought. "So then I told her that she seemed to be over-reacting and I brought up the whole crying over spilt milk thing."

"Even less smart, Daniel."

"Again you are correct. At that point we looked at each other and we both knew it was over. I packed a bag, kissed Carrie good-bye, and left for good."

"Remind me not to leave any uncovered glasses in the ice box," Sharon smiled.

"Remind me to keep my big, fat mouth shut," Daniel responded as they embraced and kissed on the dock of that bay.

Later that same evening, the time Daniel had been dreading finally arrived. He knew, instinctively, that he had another assignment. *This was the phone-call you can't hide from,* Daniel thought.

As they stood in a farewell embrace, Puma rubbing against their shins, Daniel felt truly sad.

"Are you coming back?" Sharon asked.

"Coming back, of course I am! I wish I didn't have to go."

"I'll be here, and the answer is Audrey Richards."

Daniel was confused by her words as he began to dematerialize, then remembering he smiled and was gone.

Sharon walked over to her bay window and looked down on the river. "I kind of miss him already," Sharon said. She picked up her cat and hugged her. "Don't you agree, Puma?"

The feline meowed and Sharon took it as an affirmative. Sharon had always spoken to Puma and though she didn't consider herself an eccentric cat lady, she did feel that pets could sense their owner's thoughts and emotions.

Not wanting to be alone Sharon decided to go visit Professor Templeton. As she was putting on her jacket there was a knock on her door.

"Hello Professor," she said as she opened the door. "I was just coming to see you."

"Good evening, Sharon", he responded as she let him in. "I guess great minds do think alike."

He looked around and asked, "Is Daniel here?"

"No he is on an assignment," she answered. Anticipating his question she then said, "It just comes to him, no specifics or warning, just *it's time to go*."

Spending the next few hours in pleasant conversation, the potentially miserable evening was turning into a very enjoyable one. Professor Templeton was very excited as he explained his ideas of *movement* in Heaven. "I believe that one consciously thinks the place and general time. By general time I mean an approximation. It can't be 12 noon on January 1st, that's too specific, and since time in Heaven only exists within ones existence that time and date has no meaning. Instead one would think *Sharon at her house*. If that time/location is possible one would appear with Sharon at her house. Some other force, God if you will, provides the exact time."

"I guess that would explain why Daniel arrived in my time/space so easily," Sharon agreed. "But why did it take so long for you to find me?"

"I've thought about that also. I don't think it was the correct time until it was the correct time." He smile and continued, "I'm not just fudging my answer, Sharon. I really believe there is a force in here that ensures when, where and how we meet up. That force, God if you will—though I'm not completely sure about that—allowed us to meet." He said with conviction. "I think that force, God, exists and orchestrates, to some extent, existence in Second Life. Of course, that force, God, only existed in our faith in First Life."

As he was speaking a strange feeling came over Sharon. Puma, who had been catnapping at her feet awoke and wandered into the bedroom.

"Excuse me Professor, but I think I should see what that rascal is getting into," She said as she got up to follow the cat.

"I should be going anyway," the Professor said.

Sharon did not really want to be alone so she said, "Why don't you make yourself comfortable for a minutr and I'll be right back to say good-by if you still feel like leaving." Sharon then turned her attention to her bedroom. *Maybe Daniel came back*, she thought hopefully.

Those thoughts were dashed as she felt someone roughly grab her arm. She knew instantly that this was an attack and that she should just disappear, but she thought about the Professor and Puma and hesitated for an instant. She recognized this as a horrible mistake when she felt something ropelike wrap around her arm. Trying to disappear she became terrified when nothing happened.

All of this occurred in a manner of seconds and when she truly grasped her vulnerability she decided to face her attacker. But she almost became ill when she felt, more than heard, a gravely voice right next to her head say, "I got you bitch."

The heat of his breath didn't burn her skin but it scorched her soul. *Enough is enough* she thought and using all of her strength she kicked in the direction, she hoped, of her attacker's manhood. She knew she had connected when the man grunted and dropped like a stone. Sharon realized she was somehow attached to the man when she was dragged down with him. She reached for the restraint on her arm but found it impossible to remove. It was tied or secured in some manner and it grasped her arm like a vice. The harder she tried to remove it the tighter it gripped. There was no way she was going to be able to get away.

"Fucking whore," gravely voice spewed and then slapped Sharon across the face. "Try that again and I'll break your neck." He then yanked her to her feet by her hair. Sharon couldn't stop the pain-caused tears from welling up in her eyes, but she did hold back from crying out when she heard the Professor call her from the next room.

"Is everything okay," the Professor asked?

She sensed, no, she knew, that her assailant was not going to let anyone help her and that the Professor was in grave danger.

"I'll be right out," she shouted.

"Are you sure?" He asked as his voice got closer to her bedroom door.

"Yes," she snapped! "I'll be right out." She felt horrible yelling at the Professor like that but she had to keep him away.

"That's a good girl," her captor whispered.

She wanted to claw his eyes out but she restrained herself. Not out of fear for own safety but for the safety of her friends.

Sharon looked down and saw Puma looking up at her.

"Good-bye," she said as the surrounding environment began to shimmer then disappear.

Chapter 14

"Danny Boy, it is great to see you old friend." The enthusiasm in his partner's voice made Daniel feel really good.

"It's good to see you also, Constable Gale," Daniel replied after he had fully materialized. It was fairly hot and Daniel could feel beads of sweat forming on his face. He looked over at his partner and saw that his uniform was as meticulous as ever, though he was in shirt sleeves and was not wearing a jacket. "You take me to the most beautiful places William."

"You hated the cold on Everest and now you are too hot," Gale responded with a smile. "There really is no pleasing you."

"I liked Barbados," Daniel replied.

"I liked the Guinness," Gale said as they thought about the time in that Caribbean bar.

They were in the middle of a dusty road, surrounded by clap-shackle, wooden buildings. If not for the run down pickup truck the town would have been the spitting image of an old Wild West ghost town. Which it kind of was, Daniel realized as the *knowledge* of their assignment came to him. Their current time/place was Goldfield, Nevada circa 1946.

"I know this place," Daniel said to Gale as the two Guardians walked down the road towards the setting the sun. "I remember watching a television show…" He stopped himself when he remembered that he was speaking to a man who had died nearly a century before television became a ubiquitous part of existence.

"I know of which you speak, Danny Boy," Gale seemed to read his thoughts. "I have never owned one but I have certainly been exposed to one or two in my time in Heaven. As a matter of fact I remember one of my assignments calling it an idiot box. I had no idea what he meant so I did some research. Quite frankly, I found it remarkable, not idiotic at all. The idea that information and entertainment could be found in a little electrical box is astounding."

"I guess it was a little of both, idiotic and astounding. Some of the shows that passed for entertainment during my life were absolutely ridiculous. Of course some of the images I saw on television were incredible." Daniel smiled at his friend and then continued with his original train of thought. "Goldfield was a gold mining boom town during the early 20th century in America. The Boss of the Town"—Daniel could not recall his name—"used the money he made from his gold mine to build the most opulent hotel in Nevada."

"That must be our destination," Gale interjected, "the Goldfield Hotel."

"Must be," Daniel said. "The Goldfield hotel was featured in the show I watched. It was supposed to be one of the most haunted places in America—so much so that many psychics believed it to be a portal to the afterlife." Daniel added quickly, "If you believed in such things, which I didn't, at the time." Daniel did find it somewhat ironic that he had been skeptical about almost everything during his life, especially considering where he was now.

"Ghost and spirits were a big part of society during my life, also," Gale said. "Séances were very big at parties and it was true with all levels of society. Our assignment is not a ghost in the traditional sense but he does haunt the Goldfield."

"Private First Class Joshua Hunter, U.S. Army Air Corp," Daniel explained as if reading their case information. "He died in 1944 when his B-29 was shot down over France. He was 20 years old."

"That was World War II," Daniel said again not knowing if Gale had any knowledge of that time in history he continued. "If you combined the American Revolution, The Napoleonic Wars, The Boar Wars"—Daniel couldn't think of any other British wars that had occurred before or while Gale was alive—"multiply them by 100 and you will begin to approach the scope of World War II."

"I know something of it," Gale said. "Your country and mine were on the same side and we won. Is that correct?"

"Well we won but with over 30 million dead in just a few years there were no real winners," Gale answered.

The sun was just setting when they reached a very large, brick building. "Goldfield Hotel," Gale said looking at the sign over the front door. "Private Hunter lived in this hotel when he was training. All of the enlisted bomber crews training at the nearby airfield stayed here. I guess he learned of the *other worldly* nature of this place during that time." Daniel could imagine a bunch of rambunctious young men kidding around about ghosts and spirits.

"On the day he died," Daniel said, "Hunter learned that his wife had given birth to a little girl—his little girl," Daniel paused a second as thoughts of Carrie entered his mind. "He came here almost immediately upon his death hoping he could get back to the world he had left and catch a glimpse of his baby."

"So much sadness in life and so much sadness in death," Gale said as they entered the hotel.

The only light in the lobby was the opaque sunlight coming through the dirt-encrusted windows. It had the look and feel of a haunted hotel but the only thing on Daniel's mind was finding Private Hunter.

"I do not believe that the young man is dangerous," said Gale. "So we should each look in a different area."

"Sounds good," Daniel agreed. "You take the high road and I'll take the low road…"

"And I'll be in Scotland afore ye." Gale sang in response. He continued humming the as he climbed the grand stairway to the second floor.

Heading toward the back of the building Daniel walked down a hallway stopping to listen at each doorway he passed. About half way Daniel clearly heard voices behind the door. He could make out at least two different speakers, one male the other female.

"If there is someone here please make yourself known," Daniel heard the woman say. "We aren't here to hurt you. We just want you to do something so we know you exist."

Slowly Daniel turned the door handle and as gently as possible he began to push the door open.

"Did you hear that?" Daniel could hear some real fear in the woman's voice.

"Shit yes, I think the door is opening," said the man. "Who's there?" His voice cracked a little.

As he entered the room Daniel could see a man and woman crouching in the corner. The man was holding a camera pointed at Daniel and the woman was shining her flashlight, also on Daniel. It dawned on Daniel that they could not see him and then he had to pause and take a breath when he realized the truth of what was happening. Private Hunter was right; this hotel was a portal between worlds. And these two people were looking for ghosts, and Daniel was the ghost.

"Who the hell opened that door," the woman said.

"I have no freak'n idea, Lucy. Whoever is there please understand that we mean you no harm. If you could please try to write a message on the paper we have set up on that easel we would appreciate it."

Next to the woman there was an easel set up with a large pad of paper and on the tray was a magic marker. *What the hell*, Daniel thought. He decided to give them something to appreciate or at least contemplate.

Trying to pick up the marker Daniel couldn't grasp it—his hand went right through it. But not one to give up easily Daniel summoned all of his mental strength and concentrated on the marker. As he did so he noticed the flashlight the woman was holding dimmed a little.

"Oh my God, I'm freezing," said Lucy.

"Me too," the man responded. "It's as if all of the heat was taken from the room."

Success, Daniel thought as he felt his fingers grip the marker and he lifted it up. At that instant he heard a scream and someone fell to the floor. He hoped whoever fainted was all right.

"I don't know if this is real but I'm filming it," said the man.

Daniel began to write on the paper. He felt his strength ebbing and the marker fell through his fingers. Deciding that he had had enough being a ghost, Daniel return to the land of the dead and left the room.

As he closed the door he heard the man yell, "Trust me, I will."

"Danny-boy, where are you?" Daniel heard Gale from the front room.

"Coming, William," he shouted back.

When he returned to the front room Daniel could see Gale and another man standing by the front door. Gauging by his army uniform Daniel figured that Gale had found Private Hunter.

"I guess I did get there before ye," Gale said smiling. "Daniel this is Joshua Hunter." Hunter nodded silently.

"Are you okay, Daniel, you look a little shaken," William sounded concerned.

"No I'm fine," Daniel responded, figuring he would tell him later about his *ghostly* encounter. "Let's go." As soon as he said it the three men began to disappear.

They were not going to central booking though. When they reappeared they were on the front stoop of a small bungalow type house in a suburb of, as Daniel knew, Raleigh, North Carolina.

"Where have you taken me," said Private Hunter in a distinctive southern accent.

"Why don't we knock and find out," Gale responded.

A woman answered the door and Gale asked, "Mrs. Charlotte James?"

"Yes sir."

"Well Mrs. James may I present Mr. Joshua Hunter, your father."

"Daddy," she screamed as she ran and hugged him. "Momma and I have searched all of Heaven for you after I passed on."

"Oh Charlotte, I'm so sorry I wasn't there for you," Private Hunter said through his tears.

"Nonsense Daddy, you were and are a hero in my eyes and you are here for me now."

While the two embraced Daniel whispered to Gale, "I have to tell you something important."

"Well we are finished here Danny Boy. Come to my home on Lambert Street and I'll introduce you to my lovely Elizabeth."

Daniel nodded in the affirmative and the two begin to disappear leaving the father and daughter to catch up on decades of hugs.

Chapter 15

Daniel felt extremely satisfied as he departed Private Hunter's new found existence. The result was so rewarding that Daniel hoped that most of the cases from all of the other untold Guardians in Heaven were of the same ilk as Joshua Hunter's. To have the ability to assist a troubled soul find his way was just compensation for the risk he took and time he spent as a Guardian.

"You must be happy to see me," Gale said noticing Daniel's smile as he appeared.

"Always William," you are sunshine on a rainy day.

"Never mind that," Gale said. "Please accept my heartfelt welcome to Lombard Street, in the Parrish of Lamb's Church. He tipped his hat and gracefully bowed.

"It's quite nice," Daniel said as he took in the scene around him. "They must have paid police officers a lot more in your time than they did in mine."

The houses were beautifully maintained mini-Victorians. Not giant houses by any means but beautifully maintained none-the-less. The colors were surprising to Daniel. He noticed yellow, dark blue and even purple houses. Not the typical gray siding with black shutters that he had grown used to in the tract homes that permeated Daniel's time.

"No Danny-boy we were not well compensated, by any stretch of the imagination. But my sweet Elizabeth came from wealthy parents and our house was part of the dowry. Of course I would have married her no matter what. Even if all she brought was bedlam from Finsbury Square."

Gale laughed heartily so Daniel joined in though he didn't really know what he was laughing at.

They began walking down the tree-lined street. Daniel didn't notice many people but darkness was setting and he noted some lights going on in the windows. He was too embarrassed to ask Gale if they had electricity or candles.

"Wow, where's Tiny Tim?" Daniel said when the gas streetlights illuminated, as if to add an exclamation point to the atmosphere. Gale looked somewhat bemused and didn't respond. Which made sense considering that Tiny Tim was not created until long after Gale had passed on to this world.

One thing did bother Daniel—actually the absence of something—and he wanted to ask Gale but didn't want to seem crass. Curiosity getting the best of him, Daniel asked, "William, where's the filth?"

"As you know Daniel, we left many of the more mundane and earthly aspects of life behind when we departed the old world for this. The part of the life that I miss the least is trash and other human debris." He smiled at Daniel. "No more trash piles, no rotting garbage and best of all no more pestilence ridden cesspits."

Daniel shook his head in acknowledgement. He was beginning to learn—not understand, but learn—how things worked here. He also realized that he still had much to learn. With that in mind he stopped and said to Gale. "William, may I ask you a question?"

"Of course my boy."

"Why are there so few children in Heaven?" Daniel asked. "I've seen plenty of adults and even young adults, but very few young children."

"Your bonnie lass Miss Sharon might be the better person to ask," Gale responded.

"We were so busy and it never came up."

"That doesn't surprise me," Gale said with a knowing nod. "Well here is what I believe, for what it is worth."

"As humanity progressed the age at which most people died became larger and larger. Of course I'm not considering biblical times when it seemed everyone seemed to live past the century mark. During the so called *Dark Ages* few people ever saw their 25th birthday. During my time if a person reached 50 he was considered lucky and of advanced age." He then asked Daniel, "And what constituted old age during your time? 65?"

"Well most people retired at 65," Daniel answered. "But the average life expediency in developed countries was 75 plus, it was much lower in societies that didn't have good medical care."

"Yes," Gale sighed. "Life was always easier for the have's and so much harder for the have not's."

"This is all interesting; William, but I don't see what life span has to do with your theory about children?"

"With regard to children, you see that fewer children actually died as time progressed. People who die as adults come here as adults. Additionally, and I have no real prove for this idea, but I believe that people who die young and dare I say, innocent, bypass this life and go on to another. Don't ask me where?"

"Don't worry," Daniel said as calmly as possible. "I really don't want to think about a Heaven for Heaven."

They began walking again and Daniel asked William, "Do you know how many people were living on Earth when you died?"

"No I am not sure how many."

"It was around one billion. But just a couple hundred years later when I lived, it was around seven billion!"

"Where did you all fit?" William asked not expecting an answer.

They stopped in front of a lovely yellow house. On the porch Daniel could see an attractive middle-age looking woman.

"My sweet Lizzie," Gale said as they decorously embraced.

"Welcome home Mr. Gale and welcome to your guest," she said to the men.

Gale made the introduction and Daniel bowed awkwardly in what he thought was the proper Victorian greeting. "None of that," Elizabeth Gale said kissing him on his cheek.

The inside of the house looked exactly as Daniel thought it might. He had, of course, never been inside a mid-nineteenth century home but Deb, during their marriage, had dragged him to enough antique shops that he did knew what to expect.

"May I get you some tea?"

"I think a pint of stout would be better," Gale answered. Daniel nodded in the affirmative when Elizabeth asked him if he also wanted a beer.

The warm beer tasted okay to Daniel but he would rather have had a cold frosty one instead. He easily understood why William and Elizabeth chose to live in the 19th century, eschewing some of the more modern conveniences. They live in Heaven—Second Life as Daniel was thinking of it more and more—the way they lived on Earth.

Familiarity of place *and time* is the most comfortable. As a Guardian, William had experienced many of the inventions of later times but when ever he came home he came home to the world he knew and loved.

Of all the billions—Daniel remembered Philip McKenzie

saying over 120 billion—who had died many, if not most, probably lived exactly as they had on Earth. For those who had unhappy or tragedy filled lives on Earth, Daniel hoped that in Heaven, Second Life, their existence was better. And, as Daniel had seen first hand, many people who had lived evil or sordid lives on Earth continued their turpitude in Heaven. He didn't know what percentage but he surmised that it was high.

Watching his friend sipping his stout holding his beloved Elizabeth's hand, Daniel conjectured that one's happiness on Earth was paramount in determining how where and when one lived Heaven.

As if reading his thoughts Elizabeth asked, "Have you had much time with Sharon?" She smiled maternally, "William told me that she was a lovely soul and that you were quite smitten with her."

Daniel almost spat out his beer at the word smitten. "Yes Elizabeth, I would say we are smitten with each other.

"Good on you, Danny-boy," Gale said. "You definitely need a good woman to help you while away the days here in the hereafter."

"By the way you said you would tell me later what happened at the hotel. Well, now is later so what happened?" William said to Daniel.

Daniel explained everything that had occurred, though he left out the part about writing a message.

Elizabeth weighed in. "In life we thought how great it would be to contact the dead but being dead I had never thought about contacting the living."

"Maybe that's what God wants," William said. "After-all he has kept Heaven a secret, though it was the worst-kept secret, for all of man's history."

"Plus if people really knew what was in store for them when

they died I think society would break down," Daniel added. What Earth would be like if every inhabitant knew for sure that there was a Heaven was interesting to contemplate

"Oh my God," Elizabeth shouted when she thought about the ramifications. "Many mothers would kill themselves when a beloved child died. People would become reckless and self control would vanish."

Daniel didn't know if it would be total pandemonium but he knew life on Earth would be dramatically different. They discussed it a little further and agreed there was no reason to act on what they knew. They didn't swear each other to secrecy but they also decided to only tell those closest to them.

Changing the subject Daniel asked, "Who passed on first of the two of you?"

"My William did," Elizabeth responded. "The family was heartbroken but the sickness had so ravaged his body that death seemed a relief. Isn't that so William?"

"I was ready to die," William answered.

"You would not have recognized him, Daniel," Elizabeth continued. "He weighed no more than eight stone and he couldn't even raise his head off his pillow."

Daniel found it hard to believe that the healthy, hearty man before him had been brought so low by disease.

"As I took my last breath," said Gale, I remember Elizabeth wiping my head with a damp cloth." Daniel noticed Elizabeth tighten her grip on his hand with these words. "And as my eyes closed I heard her say 'Sleep now my dear husband, I will be with you soon.'"

"And it was a good thing I was," Elizabeth said lightening the mood. "Even Heaven has temptations."

The love between the Gales that was born on Earth was easily carried into Heaven. For Daniel a love was born in Heaven that he never found on Earth. He smiled at the thought.

For the next few *days* Daniel became immersed, and enjoyably so, in the world of his partner. The Gales had ten children in life and what was a rarity of the time, they all made it to adulthood. Eight of the ten married and in turn produced forty grandchildren. Those forty grandchildren gave the Gales over 100 great grandchildren—though the patriarch and matriarch did not live long enough to see all of them born.

It was fascinating to watch Elizabeth and William work on their family tree. Unlike on Earth where the ancestry was traced from the leaves backwards, in Heaven the Gales were the roots and were looking forward. They were glad to share with Daniel a multitude of family stories, from the Grandson who became a member of parliament to the granddaughter who moved with her family to the United States—the colonies as the Gales called them. And the supply of stories was never ending with additions coming as often as their progeny passed on to this new existence.

"I always believed in Heaven," Gale said to Daniel as they said on his porch watching the world not go by. "But I thought it would be as some of the religous said, an eternity of singing Hosanna and worshipping our maker."

"Well, to be honest," Daniel retorted, "I didn't really believe that anything happened after we died. I just thought death was the end. But, when I was in the right mood and I thought there might be a Heaven I thought it would be similar to what you thought—very, very boring to say the least."

"Yes, so boring," exclaimed Gale. "Luckily it is so much more than we thought. Of course it was presumptuous of us to think we had any idea what the creator had created."

"Human folly could be found in deed and thought," Daniel said.

"Danny-boy, why don't you go get Sharon and bring her here. I am sure she and Elizabeth would get along remarkably well."

"Now?" Daniel asked. "Don't you think we should check with your wife? She might have plans."

Gale laughed. "There are no schedules in Heaven. There are no dates or appointments."

"Everything is the here and now," Daniel said in agreement. "I'll be back when you see me."

"Exactly Danny-boy, exactly," Gale said as Daniel began to disappear.

Chapter 16

"Hi Puma," Daniel said as he bent down to pet Sharon's cat. He was surprised and a little disappointed that Sharon was not there to greet him on his appearance. Of course he couldn't think of a reason why she should be—*after all she had her own death to live*, he thought.

He walked around, not snooping, but trying to learn more about the woman he now knew he loved. Most of the books were related to her field though he also found a lot of books on Germany and World War II. He was not surprised by this considering what she had been through. On her desk was a copy of a book entitled; *Observations upon the Prophecies of Daniel and the Apocalypse of St. John.* Daniel was surprised to see it was written by Isaac Newton. Opening the book there was an inscription on the front cover:

Sharon,

In life I was able to describe God's laws of physical motion but never His greatest mysteries. I tried with this book and other writings but they always eluded me. I believed then as I believe now that it is the perfection of God's works that they are all done with the greatest simplicity. He is the God of order and not of confusion.

So until we meet again to discuss the unknowable I remain,

Your friend,
Isaac Newton

Puma shocked him a little when she jumped on the desk and meowed at him. "What do you want? I'd give it to you if you could tell me." He patted her head and continued looking around.

He wasn't worried, he had no reason to be, but he did want to find her so he thought about where she might be. The obvious place to start was Professor Templeton's. Daniel decided to walk the short distance to his home.

"Hello Daniel," the Professor said cheerily when he opened the door. "Come in," he said as he stepped aside to let Daniel enter. "Where's Sharon," he asked when he saw she was absent.

"That's what I was hoping you would know," Daniel responded. "I was at her home and Puma was there but no Sharon."

The Professor became concerned and it showed on his face. "I know time has no real meaning here in Second Life, but three days ago, in my time that is, I was visiting with Sharon. She went to her bedroom for some reason or another. When she didn't return right away I went to check on her. When I asked if she was okay she responded very unSharon-like and basically told me to leave." The Professor's countenance went from concern to distress.

"Have you been back since then?" He asked with his own concern rising.

"Yes, a few times, but she was never home. I just assumed she was with you or traveling. I should not have left when she told me to. I should have checked on her to make sure she was not in distress." The Professor was the one who looked to be in distress and Daniel tried to soothe his nerves. "There was nothing for you to be concerned about. She was in her own bedroom."

"Still that's twice I did not do right by that wonderful young lady."

"That's enough, Professor," Daniel said sternly. "We have to figure this out and we don't need our thoughts clouded by things that have no bearing."

They both became silent and Daniel thought about the thought process when he traveled in Heaven. If he was going on a mission he just thought about the mission and went to where he was supposed to be. That was definitely divine intervention. When he traveled to his boat he just thought about his boat and he was there. When he had visited Sharon for the first time he just thought about Sharon at her home and he was with Sharon at her home.

"Oh shit," he said quite loudly drawing a strange look from the Professor.

This last time he had just thought *Sharon's home*, not *Sharon at her home*. Maybe if he thought that… Without hesitation he did so and nothing happened. So because Sharon was not at her home when he thought *Sharon at her home* he didn't go there.

Back on Earth he would put out a B.O.L.O. to find someone who was missing. Of course back on Earth he would have just called her on the phone. Of course, if he had called her when she was alive she might have been quite confused considering he was only two when Sharon had died.

"Professor, do you have any idea how to find someone in Heaven, err Second Life?"

"Unfortunately not, Daniel," he responded dejectedly. "I think you need place and person to find an individual." He furrowed his brow as if a light was going on in his head. "I do believe that some other force needs to make the all thing work. It is as if this force interprets your thoughts to get you where you want to go. If we had full control I would have found Sharon long before I did."

Daniel agreed that something else was needed to have a complete meeting. Sharon had told him that she had many times walked the short distance to the Professors house—even though she had no way of knowing he had died—and it was always vacant. She had not broken in but had peeked in the window. The things she saw were as she had remembered but they seemed more like set pieces from a play than the actual items.

"We need Heaven's version of LoJack," Daniel said forgetting that the Professor would have no idea what he was talking about.

Ignoring the after-his-time reference the Professor asked if Daniel could use his Guardian powers to find her.

"We don't really seem to have any special powers except the ability to detain and transport a suspect." He was beginning to feel helpless and punched his fist into his hand.

If Sharon had been aware of someone trying to kidnap her why didn't she just disappear? Maybe she wasn't kidnapped. Maybe she had been taken by a Guardian. Though for the life of him he could not come up with any conceivable reason why. Maybe it was a bad Guardian. Daniel had been aware of plenty of rogue cops while alive. Guardians transport suspects with their hands, they have no special tools or magic handcuffs. The woman he had saved in the fortress had been held by some kind of tether. That's what the two thugs had when they attacked his boat. *They weren't after me they were after Sharon.* Maybe they were in some kind of cult or gang, the men on the boat, the castle.

Was that just a coincidence? Maybe it was, but he had to check it out.

"Daniel, can you hear me?" the Professor said.

All he had thought was *Sharon at the castle*, no castle name or anything, but it must have been correct because as the Professor was speaking Daniel was already disappearing.

Chapter 17

As she was being forcibly taken from her existence Sharon felt a little regret at not fighting harder. She had never been one to back down from anything but she knew that resistance posed a greater risk to her friends than its chances of success. But now that they were safe Sharon steeled herself for the fight that was coming. She wasn't afraid and as Dylan Thomas instructed; *Do not go gentle into that good night. Rage, rage against the dying of the light.*

They reappeared in a very large room festooned with banners and flags. The walls were lined with medieval weapons of all sorts including mazes, spears, swords and battle-axes. The only illumination in the room came from two narrow windows high up the wall and a plethora of candles—some in wall sconces and some in candelabras on tables scattered throughout the room. The room had a seedy and sooty dimness that caused a chill to run down her spine.

"New meat," her captor shouted out. He then looked at Sharon and laughed maniacally. He grabbed Sharon's arm and she instinctively tried to fight him off. She was able to shed his hand but as she did so the tether tightened to the point that it caused her pain. "And she's a fighter," her captor said as he grasped Sharon's hair and thrust her forward into the haze.

A foul odor—smoke mixed with dampness—permeated the air. There was also an undercurrent of moaning and crying that told Sharon that she was not the only captive. As her eyes adjusted to the gloom Sharon felt that she was no longer in the Heaven she knew. The dystopia before her reminded her of the description of the Nazi Death Camps she had heard from her grandparents. A fate she had so narrowly avoided non Earth.

Around the room men of all types were seated in large wingback chairs. Many were smoking and drinking and all seemed rowdy and boisterous. Attached to each man by a tether was a woman, and like the men they were all from different times and places from history.

"Have a seat," her captor said. "We don't get our turn until we're selected by the Countess." At the mention of a Countess, Sharon couldn't help but look at her captor quizzically.

"Yes Countess Elizabeth Bathory," the man responded. "This is her home, the castle Csejth. Have you heard of her?"

Sharon shook her head no and the man continued. "The Countess was known as the Vampire of Romania. She liked to play with young women and sometimes the play got a little rough. She killed hundreds and her legend grew. Rumor had it that she used to bath in their blood to keep her skin young." He laughed and spittle ran down his chin. Sharon held back her gag reflex but it wasn't easy. "But the rumors were not true," he continued. "She just hacked them up so nicely that she became covered in their blood." This time he laughed so hard that he went into a paroxysm of coughing.

"Maybe that kept her young but what really kept her from getting old was that they entombed her alive. Ain't that right

Teddy," he said to the youngish and very handsome man sitting near them.

"I guess if you are implying that her death at such a young age kept her legend fresh you are probably correct. Her situation was not dissimilar to my own. Both of us were struck down long before our full glory was realized." The man named Teddy had sounded so erudite that Sharon was taken aback.

"That's our Teddy," her captor said quietly. "He'll talk your ears off before he cuts your head off." And then again the terrifying laugh.

Except for the despondent sobbing the room fell silent when a door opened at the top of the stairs. A woman regally descended into their room and even through the darkness Sharon could see that she was a real enchantress. As if addressing a room full of school boys she said, "Oh how nice, my boys have brought me a room full of presents." Her smile was horrifically beautiful. "You are all too good to me."

She walked around the room pausing to caress some of *her boy's* heads. *Her boys*, Sharon thought sardonically. The men in this room were mostly brutish louts and yet they nodded and bobbed like little puppies when the Countess touched them. It seemed strange to Sharon that the Countess had such control over them. It was obvious that any one of these men, excepting, maybe, the one named Teddy, could break the petite countess's neck without even straining. The captive women, on the other hand, seemed to shrink with fear, trying to become invisible to the Countess's scrutiny.

The Countess stopped in front of the man she now knew as Teddy. Attached to him Sharon saw a young woman dressed in oriental garb, reminiscent of a courtesan of Imperial China. "A daughter of Ming," the Countess said as she stroked the young girl's face. "Come Ted, tonight we visit the Forbidden City."

Grabbing the girl roughly Teddy followed the countess back up the stairs. It wasn't long after the door was slammed shut that the screaming began.

"I so love it here," her captor said to no one in particular. Then turning to Sharon he said "Well, young lady since we will soon be joining the Countess allow me to introduce myself."

He told Sharon that he was Benjamin Johnson. He had been born in London but had been sentenced to a life of hard labor in the penal colony in New South Wales. He laughed and Sharon cringed when he told her his crime had been murder and sodomy.

"I should have been for the gallows but they judge showed mercy. Though I think his mercy was because he was short on his deportation numbers. And who might ye be?"

Sharon ignored the question and said, "So you are lapdogs to that witch and you risk eternal damnation to serve her?" She didn't expect an answer but got one anyway.

"We know the risks, but goddamit if the Countess don't seem immune to any punishment. We've lost a few men but the coppers don't seem very organized. Besides there are always more men to replace the ones we lose." He went on to explain how the men travel from time/place to time/place looking for recruits and for women. Everything is random and to him the hunt was as fun as the capture.

Sharon wanted to tell him that her boyfriend was one of those *coppers*, who would not hesitate to send the whole lot of them to Hell. But instead she asked, "What are these tethers?"

"That's a Devil's leash," he said. "We don't know where the Countess gets them but when a man proves his worth she gives him one of his own. It's our badge of honor and means we are part of this very special Heavenly society." He laughed at his own sarcasm.

"Once we are linked you can't escape," he continued. "That is unless you can get the leash out of my grip. That's why I don't just hold it; I attach it to my arm also." He lifted his left arm to show Sharon the leash wrapped around his forearm.

"Go ahead, try to get away. I know you want to," he taunted.

Knowing that she probably wouldn't be able to severe the link Sharon tried anyway. No matter how hard she tried to pry the leash off of her arm it just seemed to get tighter.

"Don't waste your strength," he said just as a new set of screams emanated from the room upstairs. "You are going to need it."

The fear that Sharon felt might have lessened a little if she knew that Daniel was now hiding just a few feet from where she sat.

He had appeared in a dark corner and sensing a people around him he had scrambled behind a drape. Ensconced behind the drapery and realizing he had not been seen he peered out from his hiding place to get a look at the room. He had no idea if it was the same castle he had been in before with Gale but that didn't matter. As he tried to differentiate between the voices he is a little startled when the room falls silent as a door opens from up the stairs.

He caught glimpses of a smallish woman walking down the steps and heard fragments of what she said; "My boys…" "Forbidden City…" "Come Ted…"

He clearly heard the screams that came a few minutes later. A couple of minutes passed when Daniel heard a voice that he clearly recognized as Sharon's. He spied into the room and by following the voice he was able to pick out Sharon in the gloom.

His first instinct was to rush out guns a blazing. His policeman's instinct told him that that metaphorical approach would be a foolish. He began a more thorough examination of the surrounding area. While he did so he heard Sharon and her captor discussing the Devil's Leash and then he stopped to listen as she tried to get away. When the struggling was over and he was pretty sure that Sharon was not hurt he began looking around again.

Along the wall he could see many weapons including swords and axes. They seemed to be lined up ready for use, like firemen's boots waiting for action in a firehouse.

He tried to gage the distance from where he was to the weapons and then to Sharon. It was ten feet, at most. The most important appraisal came next—could he cover that distance before he was seen or heard? No other people were located between the weapons and Sharon. He should be able to make it providing he didn't trip or drop something. And when he got there, what then? Kill the bad guy? Grab Sharon and hope his Guardian powers were stronger than the Devil's Leash?

Analyzing time ended abruptly when Daniel heard the door upstairs open. The time to act was now. Edging to the weapons he had decided on the ax before he got there. He briefly regretted that choice when he picked it up and found how heavy it was. The beefiness of the ax did mean it would do plenty of damage. Of course that would depend on Daniel being able to swing it.

Step by step he inched his way toward Sharon. As he crept he also raised the ax to the striking position.

"We are almost finished up here." The woman's voice was coming from upstairs. *This was good,* he thought. Most attention would now be focused on her and he should be able strike before being noticed. He caught Sharon's eyes as he stealthily approached. She didn't make a sound but he did notice a glimmer of hope and expectation appears. He knew he would save her or die trying. Those were the only two options. Taking a deep breath he swung the ax downward as hard as he could. With a sickening thud he could feel the ax pierce skin, sinew and bone. He then felt the shock of the impact all the way to his shoulder as the ax split the wood of the chair's arm. As the ax stopped Daniel heard a blood curdling scream that reverberated throughout the room and echoed off the stone walls.

He gently took hold of Sharon's shoulder and thought *William at his home.* Nothing!

"Daniel, the leash," Sharon screamed.

"Shit." He said as he saw that the leash was still attached to the man's forearm and though the forearm was completely detached from the rest of the arm he was holding it with his good arm. Before he could act Daniel saw Sharon grab the leash with both of her hands. She pulled as hard as she could and was able to yank the severed arm out of the man's hand. As soon as he saw this he thought of William at his home again and this time the room shimmered and they disappeared.

Chapter 18

William's smile lasted less time than it took for Daniel and Sharon to fully materialize. "I dare say, Daniel! What is that?" Gale said pointing to the severed arm that was still attached to the Devil's Leash, which was still attached to Sharon.

Daniel pulled on the leash and it separated from Sharon. "That's better," she said rubbing her arm. He let it fall to the ground and both he and Sharon gasped in surprise when the severed arm vanished. Gale bent down and picked up the leash. Running it through his hands he said, "I've seen plenty of strange sights in Heaven but that takes the cake."

"William that was nothing compared to where we were." Daniel said beginning a complete description of the events that had enveloped Sharon and him. His explanation was from his perspective and Sharon followed with complete details of what she had experienced. Gale stood transfixed as the story unfolded. He took in every detail silently holding his tongue on some of the more disturbing aspects even though he wanted to say something to convey his anger.

As they winded down, Elizabeth, who had been in the doorway listening to the whole tale, came running down. "Oh you poor dear," she said enveloping Sharon in a motherly hug. She led Sharon to the sofa and sat down next to her, holding Sharon's hand in both of hers.

Thank you Mrs. Gale," Sharon said assuming and hoping the woman was Mrs. Gale.

"Please call me Elizabeth." She said, and then she turned toward William. "If my big oaf of a husband had any manners he would have provided proper introductions." She then gave a gentle and loving tap to Williams's stomach.

"Well Lizzie, there was that slight matter of an unattached arm."

Elizabeth shuttered at the mention of that grisly sight. "Why did it just vanish?, she asked.

I'm not a hundred percent sure," Daniel postulated. "But I think that Devil's Leash has the power to carry whatever or whoever is attached to it from one time/place to another."

"Much like we can do as Guardians," William added.

"Well if it has that kind of power," Elizabeth said with disgust. "It has the right name because the Devil must have made it."

The four of them settled down and relaxed in the Gale's comfortable living room. Elizabeth served tea and they did their best to avoid any discussion of Sharon's recent ordeal. It was time to get to know each other as Elizabeth made quite clear.

Sharon relayed her history, as did the Gales. Much of Elizabeth's attention was on her children and grandchildren. She was telling them of Arthur, one of her grandson's who had become a full professor at Cambridge, when Daniel jumped to his feet.

"Oh my God, I forgot Professor Templeton." Turning to Sharon he asked her to stay put and then disappeared.

The Gale's looked stunned but Sharon realized instantly

where he was going. Before she had time to explain Daniel was back with the Professor

. "Sharon," the Professor exclaimed when he saw her. "I thought something dreadful had happened to you."

"I'm fine Professor, and I'll tell you all about it later."

"No need, my dear. Daniel has already filled me in."

Turning to Daniel, Sharon expressed surprise. "But you were gone for just seconds."

"Sharon," Daniel chided. "You've been in Heaven much longer than I so I'm surprised you don't realize that time…"

"Has no bearing in Heaven except within ones current existence," William and Sharon said in unison causing everyone to laugh.

Later that evening Daniel, William, and Sharon were enjoying the beautiful night's air on the Gale's front porch. Earlier, when Professor Templeton had informed the Gale's that he was very interested in Victorian life, Elizabeth insisted on an in-depth tour. She wanted him to see first hand what life, as the Gales had lived, was like.

"Daniel, we have to help those women," Sharon implored.

"I know Sharon, I just don't know how," Daniel responded sadly.

"I've been thinking on that very subject." Gale said, surprising Daniel and Sharon. Especially Daniel, who said, "I thought we had to leave things alone. You made that very clear when we were on the Bedeaux assignment."

"No Danny-boy. I said we have to stick to the task at hand. I never implied that I would not help someone who needed it. And it sounds like those ladies need it."

Daniel was gratified that Gale felt that way, justifying the very high esteem to which he held him. "Well I knew you would both want to help," Sharon said. "So what is your idea William?"

Oh no Miss Sharon. I said I've been thinking on it not that I had any ideas."

"What are your thoughts then?" Daniel asked.

"Let's review," Gale said. "We know that the brutes are serving the witch. Correct?" Sharon and Daniel both nodded their assent. "The fact that it may or may not be the castle Daniel and I and been in earlier does not really matter. Going room to room is something we can do later. For now we have to help the group of ladies being held in that hellish waiting room."

Again they nodded their agreement. With Daniel adding, "We can't just go in and free them. As much as I would like a direct frontal attack there are just too many bad guys to take that chance. We might be able to sneak in. Either way they seemed very devoted to the Countess and I think they will fight."

"If for some reason they didn't fight they can just disappear with the captives before we can help them," Gale added.

"Unfortunately both scenarios could lead to an unfortunate end for the poor women." Sharon was dispirited as she said this, sensing there might not be a viable option—one with a modicum of a chance for success—to save the captives.

The three conspirators were each in trying to figure out a way to help when Professor Templeton and Elizabeth returned. Sharon, deep in thought, gasped when she saw Elizabeth. Every eye turned towards her and embarrassed she apologized and explained. "Elizabeth you gave me a start because I thought you were Elizabeth Bathory."

"They may have the same first name," William said. "But my Elizabeth doesn't seem to have the same tastes as the Countess. And I can't for the life of me imagine confusing the two."

"Oh my God, no," exclaimed Sharon. "I didn't mean…" She turned to Elizabeth and continued. "You just look like her and she is quite beautiful." Sharon's face was now beet red.

"Does she really look like her?" Daniel asked as an idea began to germinate.

"What are you getting at Danny-boy?" William asked sensing something he wouldn't like was coming.

"The captors would not be suspicious of strangers if the Countess introduced them," Daniel answered.

Sharon spoke up before William could protest. "They might be fooled from far away but up close or if our Elizabeth spoke they would know she was an imposter."

"She wouldn't have to say anything and she could stay at the top of the stairs."

William could hold back no longer. "I will not allow my wife get involved in this dangerous scheme."

"Hush, William Gale. During our life on God's Earth I worried every day that you might not come home. You always said you were doing good work and if God took you it would be his will. So I dutifully let you do your good work but I still worried. Now that we are in God's Heaven I still have to worry you won't come home every time you go on assignment. At least on Earth I knew I would one day join you in Heaven, but I don't know how I would spend eternity without you here in Heaven. But I know without a doubt that you are doing God's work and I accept it. So now, when I am called to do God's work and save those poor girls, how can I not accept my task?"

"Elizabeth," William implored. "You have no training…"

"I said hush," Elizabeth scolded. "I will at the very least listen to Daniel."

"We will listen to Daniel," William said smiling at her. He then turned to Daniel and gave him a look that would have withered a lesser man.

So under William's glare Daniel outlined the basics of his plan. After each had his and her input they felt as if they had developed a very sound strategy with a good chance of success. Daniel hoped.

After extensive review and practice they took a short break to clear their minds. When he felt it was time to act Daniel said, "Let's have one last review. William, why don't you start?"

William cleared his throat. "Yes, okay. Daniel, the Professor and I all transport together to the Countess's room hoping she is there. If she is alone we will immediately bring her back here where we will regroup and decide what to do next."

"Correct," Daniel said. "But what if she is not alone, Professor?"

"I will use the Devil's Leash," The Professor held it up as if at a show and tell presentation, "and use it on any other girl that might be in the room."

"Except the Countess," Sharon interjected.

"Yes Sharon, except the Countess," the Professor responded somewhat annoyed at her seeming lack of faith. He thought of all the practicing he had done. They had run through scenario after scenario with Mrs. Gale acting as the Countess and Sharon playing a captive. He felt very secure in the prospect of doing his part successfully and was disheartened at Sharon's lack of faith.

"I said that that for my own edification," Sharon smiled as she said this and the Professor couldn't help but smile back. He truly loved this young lady as if she were his own daughter.

"You did great with the Devil's Leash," Daniel added. "So what happens next?" He prodded the Professor back on track.

"After I bring the freed damsel back here I calm her down and try to find out what she might know about that sordid operation. I also wait for your return."

"Perfect," Daniel said. "Now, how about you two?" He asked as he pointed to Sharon and Elizabeth.

"You tell the proctor, Sharon," Elizabeth said in a slightly mocking tone.

Sharon smiled and said, "We wait here until William comes with the Countess or the Professor comes with one of the young ladies."

"If it is William we have to hurry and I will switch clothes with her," Elizabeth took over explaining their roles. Shaking her head in dismay she said more to herself than the others, "I pray to God that she is wearing clothes." Seeing William smile she continued, "Once I am changed I join Daniel in the Countess's room."

"Correct," Daniel said. "By then I will have successfully subdued anyone else in the room." He hoped.

"I, in the meantime," William began explaining his role "will bring the Countess to Central Booking convincing someone to hold her and then join Daniel and my Elizabeth back in the other Elizabeth's room."

"Perfect," Daniel was becoming enthusiastic about the plan and was starting to believe it might work. "Once the Countess's room is secured and Elizabeth and William have joined me, Elizabeth will lead us out of the room and direct us to the stairway."

"Hopefully the men in the waiting room will think it is the Countess and that you two," Sharon said pointing to William and Daniel, "are two of her henchmen"

"It's up to us to then free the captive women and get out." Daniel's doubts about the plan returned. This was the part of the scheme that they had no idea as to how it would unfold.

"You know," Sharon said, "those man are not really paying attention to each other so I think you and William should be able to bring each captor and his captive out of the room without anyone else noticing."

"Excellent idea," William said, "I think that's exactly what we should do and take them directly to central."

"That's a lot of disappearing and reappearing but I agree it might be the only way," Daniel said not feeling any more confident.

"No time like the present," Daniel said. He stood and was followed immediately by the rest of his band of conspirators, each one determined to do the best they could and each one willing to risk his or her existence to help some people who needed help.

Chapter 19

"Let me be very clear," Daniel was very serious as he looked at each of his friends in turn. "There is real danger here and we don't need any heroes. If the plan goes south we abort, it's that simple. We all come back here without hesitation."

"To paraphrase Demosthenes; *live to fight another day.*" the Professor said.

"Or as Dumas wrote in The Three Musketeers; *One for all, all for one.*" William added.

"Unus pro omnibus, omnes pro uno," Sharon added not looking at anyone. Realizing everyone was looking at her she added, "It's Latin for one for all, all for one. I remember seeing it on the Federal Palace in Switzerland after fleeing Germany."

"Don't you have a quote to add?" Elizabeth asked Daniel. "We have Greek, French and Latin quotes, so why don't you add something from your time."

Daniel thought a moment and he remembered a very appropriate sentiment, "Let's roll." With that the Professor, William and Daniel disappeared.

A wave of emotion came over the Professor as the room shimmered. He had felt the strong, caring feelings each of his friends had for each other. He also understood that here, just as on Earth, a person's worth was measured by his deeds not his wealth or stature. And his little band of brothers and sisters were worth everything to him.

The Professor had felt nervous and excited as they discussed and practiced this rescue mission. He had always been a bookish man. He had done his part for Canada during the War but all it entailed was studying German newspapers and writings. He had never been a man of action and most people in life—and now in death—considered him somewhat of the absent-minded professor. He was very pleased that Daniel had included him in his plan and felt confident and determined to carry it our successfully. *What if my target looks like the Countess? Will I be able to tell them apart?* As they began to reappear he was now feeling more nervous than excited. The Professor wasted no time in appraising the situation. Looking first to make sure there was a hostage in the room he saw a young lady cowering in the corner. He started towards her, Devil's Leash at the ready, when he saw, no felt, Daniel blast by him. He seemingly was flying. Then with a kick, a spin, and another kick, the man, a giant of a man, who was the target of Daniel's attack, fell without so much as a whimper. No longer the menacing captor he was now a listless bundle on the floor. The Professor saw this as his chance. Snapping the leash, as he had practiced countless times before, he wrapped it around the young girl's arm. He knew he should vanish immediately but thought he might just peak around to see if he was needed. He sensibly resisted that urge and thought, *back to the Gales'*.

"You will be punished for your impertinence," were the first words he heard as he appeared back at the Gales'. They words were coming from a woman he knew to be the Countess. She was fighting like a cornered rat but when Williams applied his iron grip all she could do was squirm.

"Elizabeth" Sharon said in a high nervous voice, "hurry, take the frock." They took off the Countess's robe. The Professor noted that William disappeared with the Countess the instant the robe was off. He then saw that as soon as Elizabeth had finished slipping it on she too disappeared.

After those fleeting but action filled moments ended the Professor took a deep breath and looked around. With him in the room were Sharon and a very frightened young lady. With sympathy for her fear the Professor released the Devil's Leash. "There you go my dear," he said but before he had finished the woman was gone.

Sharon smiled at the Professor's perplexed look and said, "You did great Professor, and you can hardly blame her for fleeing. She must have been terrified. I think I probably would have done the same."

"Oh I understand that Sharon but all of these disappearings and reappearings are so discombobulating." He chuckled slightly. "It reminds me of a movie I saw when I was alive and the heroine said, if I remember correctly; *My! People come and go so quickly here!*"

"Yes I remember the movie," Sharon responded, "and I've a feeling we're not in Kansas any more."

They both laughed for a moment and then fell silent. Out of the blue Sharon said, "When I got to Heaven, Professor, you were one of the people I missed the most from my life on Earth. You were a good friend when I was alive and you are a dear friend now that I'm dead."

"Thank you Sharon," he said looking away so she wouldn't see the tears forming.

Wiping the tears and thinking, *that's the old Templeton, I am now a man of action*, he said, "I think we should go back to see if we can help," he said.

"No, Daniel said to sit tight." Changing the subject she

continued, "So you were in the Countess's room. I'm sure glad I was never there when I was in their hands. What was it like?"

"Well I didn't take note of much in the room, but let me tell you young lady. You should feel very save with Daniel. The way he took care of the brute that was in there. He was quite impressive."

"I know," she said very quietly. She then noticed how fidgety the Professor was acting and emphasized that they should stay where they were.

The Professor felt energized. Books and studying seemed a lifetime ago—as it was—and he was filled with something that he couldn't define. And he had to act.

"You wait here Sharon," he said and he was gone.

. . .

"Unus pro omnibus, omnes pro uno," Sharon said as the rescue mission was about to begin. Elizabeth turned to her friend surprised. Sharon continued, "it's Latin for one for all, all for one. I remember seeing it on the Federal Palace in Switzerland after fleeing Germany."

Then Daniel said, *Let's role*, at Elizabeth's prodding and the three men were gone.

"He's a good man," Elizabeth said noticing the loving glance exchanged between Sharon and Daniel after they had disappeared.

Sharon responded, "They all are."

"Of course, my dear, I just saw you looking at Daniel."

"I know and thank you."

That was all the time they had alone before William reappeared with the Countess. Within seconds the Professor was back with a young woman attached to the horrible Devil's Leash. Elizabeth didn't have time to spare for him as she and Sharon went to work on the Countess. The Countess was struggling ferociously but Elizabeth had no doubts about Williams's ability to hold her.

"Elizabeth" Sharon said, "Hurry, take the frock."

They removed the beautiful silk robe from the Countess who was spitting and hissing like a cobra. Sharon helped her slip the robe on and without hesitation she thought, *The Countess's room with Daniel.*

Daniel was standing there when she arrived and said more as a question than a statement, "Elizabeth, everything going okay?"

"Exactly as you planned, William," she answered. "William should be here promptly." And as she finished, he was.

"The Countess was very unhappy with her situation," William said. "Mr. Lee said he would find someone to hold her."

"Hopefully, they will," Daniel said.

Elizabeth saw that her husband was about to speak with her but was distracted by the man lying in a heap on the floor. Instead he said to Daniel, "I see you did your job. Is he dead?"

"No, but he should be out for a while." Elizabeth listened as the men discussed if they should restrain him somehow. She was about to explain that that would be fruitless when they realized that fact on there own.

Daniel then said, "You know, William, unless we kill those men," he gestured downward, "they will be right back to their same old tricks."

Elizabeth began to get a little antsy when her husband said, "At least we can help the girls they have now." Not wanting to waste any more time Elizabeth jumped in, "I don't think we will help anyone if we don't stick to the plan."

"Your right," Daniel said. Then to Elizabeth, "Are you ready."

"Ready as I will ever be," she responded without hesitation—though her voice was a little tentative.

William held her arm gently as Daniel opened the door and the three slowly left the room.

Chapter 20

As they left the Countess's room Daniel felt all of the eyes from down below turn their way. Elizabeth was in the center guiding William and Daniel by their arms. She seemed to falter slightly as they approached to the top of the stairs. Daniel heard William whisper, "You are doing great my love. I am so proud of you." Daniel felt Elizabeth's confidence return as she squeezed his arm a little bit harder. She stopped and with all of the majesty of the Queen of England she pointed down the stairs. Any observer might be expected to assume she was telling the two men to leave her presence and descend the stairway. Getting into the mood of the charade and feeling that a little more convincing might be needed—he felt unnerved by the total silence before them—Daniel adlibbed and said, "We apologize, Mistress, for our mistake. We will wait for you to call for us." Elizabeth nodded her head and took a step back.

Walking together Daniel and William began to make their way down the stairway. They were halfway down when Daniel heard extensive commotion coming from the Countess's room. Turning his head Daniel saw that Elizabeth was still standing where they had left her causing him to became instantly concerned. His concern became despair when the door slammed open like a gunshot and standing in the doorway was the Countess—the real Countess. Behind her was the brute Daniel had knocked out. *I guess I should have killed him*, he thought. He was holding a big knife and a Devil's Leash. Attached to the other end of the tether Daniel saw, to his horror, Sharon.

"Oh my lord!" William exclaimed as the Countess wielded another leash and captured his Elizabeth.

"My pets," the Countess hollered. "Our palace has been breached and we have intruders in our midst." A grumble erupted from down below followed by shuffling and scurrying.

Looking down into the room below Daniel saw a mass of men approaching the stairway. He estimated at least ten, maybe more. He was happy to notice all of the girls were no longer tethered and finding themselves unattached they disappeared as quickly as they could.

"Not the way you planned, Danny-boy," William said. "The women are free at least, so we did accomplish something."

Daniel saw William smile ever so slightly despite how distraught he must feel, so he added, "Now just two more." He gestured towards Elizabeth and Sharon telling William all he needed to know. In order to save the women they loved they would have to fight and win—they could not lose and there would be no flight.

"I guess we have a new plan," William responded as the first of the attackers reached them.

They two Guardians knew the odds were against them. Besides the fact that they were outnumbered, their attackers were all armed with the weapons Daniel had seen against the wall when he was looking for Sharon. Daniel was somewhat relieved to note that the stairway narrowed considerably right below where they were preparing to fight. Only two attackers at a time could reach them. *Of course they could teleport to the stairs above Daniel and William,* Daniel thought. He hoped that they were not that organized and would not think of anything but a frontal attack.

The first two attackers were not very big but they were armed with two very big bayonets. Daniel could tell they were not very skilled swordsmen, they were holding the blades for a slashing strike rather than a thrust—for which were designed—and he was able to relieve his attacker of his weapon with out too much effort. Then with a kick he saw the man fall backwards into the men behind him. He was glad to watch as his vanquished foe took a couple others with him as he fell. William must have had the same type of success because he was now also holding a bayonet ready for the fight to continue.

"Take you time," the countess yelled. "They are not going anywhere."

Daniel didn't look upward at the Countess; he kept his eyes focused on the advancing gang. He had no idea how long the fight was lasting, though it seemed to be flying by. His instinct controlled his actions and his training controlled his muscles. Thrusting, parrying, kicking and punching, steel against skin and fist against flesh. Blood splattered and bones crunched. His muscles ached and his lungs were screaming for air. He caught a glimpse of William and was relieved to see he was still fighting. But he did not know how much longer they could continue with this incredible exertion. Then like an explosion everything went silent.

Below them a few bodies were strewn about but Daniel realized that many of the thugs had departed before fighting or after being hurt in the fight, *so much for undying devotion to their Mistress.*

"Well done," the Countess said in a mocking tone which she was probably using to hide her disappointment. "We are at somewhat of an impasse I would say." She looked at Elizabeth and Sharon then back to William and Daniel. "We could just leave with our hostages but I think you would not rest until you found us and freed your ladies."

"Maybe we should just leave, Countess," the man holding Sharon said.

"Shut up," she snapped. "I don't want to hear your voice. You failed me." The brute of a man hung his head in shame.

"We can't let them leave," Daniel whispered to William who nodded that he understood.

"You can just leave by yourselves," William shouted so the Countess could hear him. "By the way how did you get free?"

"The mighty Guardian is surprised I escaped the clutches of your compatriots." She laughed then continued. "In life I had friends, gentlemen friends, at all levels of society. Now, in death, I still have friends everywhere, even amongst the ranks of the Guardians."

She continued, "One of my friends took me into his custody," again the laugh, "and then he set me free. When I returned I found this lout, who was supposed to be my defender, getting up from the beating one of you gave him. And then to my surprise this one appears," she gestured towards Sharon "along with a feeble old man. The old man didn't last too long."

The Countess then said to Daniel's horror, "I think we should just kill these harlots and get out of here. How does that sound, Guardians?" The Countess was a vengeful and evil woman whose death mirrored her life. As she and the man lifted their knifes ready to strike, a scream, "Noooo," erupted from out of the Countess's room and then, still screaming, came Professor Templeton running at full speed. He headed directly for the man holding Sharon. Then the Professor lowered his head like a battering ram. Unable to react quickly enough the man dropped the Devil's Leash and tried to bring his knife to bear. He was too slow and the Professor, like a bull heading for a tormenting matador, rammed his head full force into the man's stomach The force of the collision drove both men straight through the wooden banister and then over the ledge, plunging to the floor below.

Chapter 21

Silence ensued in the moments immediately after the Professors gallant charge. Concern for the Professor took hold of Daniel and he turned to head down the stairs to see if he was alright. Daniel stopped when the Countess screamed, "Enough."

Looking up he saw the Countess holding Elizabeth with a knife to her throat. She no longer had just one guard standing by her. Flanking her were at least five bodyguards. Daniel recognized some of them as men who had fled the fight when they were losing the battle but now were returning for the victory. This time the bad guys had all of the advantages. They had the high ground plus they were approaching from a wider part of the stairway—now they all could join the fight at the same time. Daniel also realized as he watched them begin to advance down the stairs that he and William were too exhausted to effectively fight these refreshed men. Never-the-less they prepared to fight to the end. Daniel took some deep, slow breaths trying to get as much oxygen into his lungs as possible.

As he was getting ready for the onslaught an idea occurred to him. If he did now what he was afraid the attackers were going to do earlier, namely, transport himself above them and attack from behind—outflank them—he might take away some of the advantages they currently held. He knew it was risky, especially since he would be leaving William alone, no matter how briefly. But he thought it might be their only chance and he was about to tell William about it when he felt a new presence next to him. He turned thinking it might be an attacker. It wasn't and he almost gagged when he saw the hideous face staring at him with her grotesque smile. "Hegate," he shouted. The smell was as recognizable as the ugliness. All activity stopped when her presence became known. Everyone, the Countess, her men, Elizabeth, Sharon and William stared open-mouthed at the terror before them. It seemed to Daniel that Hegate relished the attention she commanded and she seemed to stand a little taller—all four feet of her. Not knowing what else to do Daniel asked, "What are you doing here?"

"My boss sent me to pick that one up," her gnarled fingers pointed at the Countess who was now completely nude and frozen in place. Daniel knew that Hegate now had control of her and she was doomed. Her brave and devoted guards, on the other hand, had departed without hesitation when Hegate had cast a glance their way.

"Who is your boss?" Daniel asked almost rhetorically, figuring the answer was obvious. Maybe the countess had pledged her soul to him and he had sent Hegate to collect. He was surprised and a little disturbed when she responded, "My boss is the same as your boss." Her voice was almost normal and she smiled directly at Daniel, but not her normal, terrifying, intimidating smile, this one was almost friendly. In the next instant her actions were anything but friendly. With a shriek she left her feet and flew up the stairway and without hesitation she seized the Countess in a manner that was far beyond undignified. For someone like the Countess, who had thrived on her dominance, it must have been humiliating and very, very painful. Though Elizabeth Bathory made no sound her eyes screamed as loud as any vocal chord as they became as wide as plates when she fully realized what was about to befell her. She was on the verge of being punished with the loss of her very existence—for the second time. This was that threshold instant of no return. Daniel had no idea if the Countess had any remorse, or if she was even capable of that feeling. Though it didn't matter anymore for her fate was now irrevocably cast—for eternity.

After Hegate and the Countess had gone Daniel headed upstairs to check on Sharon. He stopped when he saw Sharon rushing down the stairs. "The Professor," she said as she ran past Daniel and William. Daniel caught up to her as she knelt by the Professor. William and Elizabeth caught up and Elizabeth gasped.

The man the Professor had attacked was gone but he had left something terrible behind. As they gently rolled the Professor over they could see the man's dagger planted in his chest up to its hilt. His eyes were lifeless and Daniel realized this was another threshold moment.—the Professor was gone. Sharon began to sob and Elizabeth held her tightly. William bent down to confirm what everyone already knew.

"His soul has moved on," William said with compassion. "We don't know what is next, just as we didn't know what came after we died on Earth. But I have faith that as our spirit leaves this existence it moves a little closer to God.

"He loved you Sharon," Daniel said. "He gave up his Earth life because he couldn't deal with the guilt of harming you. And now he gave up his existence because he couldn't bear the thought of someone harming you."

Sharon bent down and gently closed his eyes and said "What should we do with him? I won't leave him here." She was emphatic on this point.

"We don't have to do anything my dear, God will take care of it," William answered. "On Earth our bodies went back to the Earth, dues to dust, you know. But here in Heaven our souls are the only part of us that really exists and when our soul does depart our physical presence just evaporates."

That was exactly what was happening, but it wasn't instantaneous. It was a dignified and ethereal disappearing. They all stood holding hands and looking down at their friend's body as it slowly faded to nothing. Before he was completely gone Daniel said, "There will be no memorials build for Professor Templeton, but their will be memories—our memories. And when we think of him we will always know that he was a very good man who did a very great thing."

"Amen," said Elizabeth and William in unison.

Chapter 22

The four friends had not uttered a word since returning from Countess Bathory's castle. Their physical ailments and injuries had healed immediately upon arriving in the Gale's parlor. Unfortunately the sorrow they felt was not so easily cured.

"When my father died," Daniel said, finally breaking the silence, "I didn't feel any great sadness." Sharon gave him a knowing glance at this admission. "But I did feel a very strong emptiness—as if a part of me had gone and wasn't coming back." He looked around the room. "But now, with the Professor gone I just feel sad, completely sad."

"I know that emptiness of which you speak, Daniel," Elizabeth Gale said. "It is like hollowness in your stomach." Daniel nodded his concordance. "I remember it well when a kin or loved one died on Earth. But I also don't feel it now." She suddenly felt defensive. "I thought highly of The Professor, but just like you, all I feel is sad. I wonder why that is."

"It's because the emptiness we felt on Earth was caused by the anticipation of the time, the rest of our lives actually, that we would be without the loved one," Sharon said very clinically and without emotion. "We knew that there would be a hole in our lives without the deceased. That's where that hollowness comes from. I'm not sure why we don't have that same type of feeling here. It might be because we have no real sense of time. Or maybe God doesn't want us to feel empty when someone is not present any more. But I do know that the sadness, whether here or on Earth, is real and is from our soul, which we brought with us from our old life to this one." All of a sudden the tears were back. She laid her head on Daniel's shoulder and he gently stroked her hair.

"All I can say about all of this philosophical stuff," Daniel said in his best *I ain't got no book learnin* voice, "is that whoever is running this cockamamie place would be a darned fool not to welcome the Professor to the next level." He then added in as sincere a tone as he could, "And I'm sure there is a next level."

Sharon stopped crying, which was Daniel's goal, and Elizabeth and William nodded in agreement.

They all became contemplative as to what Daniel had said. The Gale's had been deeply religious people on Earth and though they no longer believed in a particular religion they were still very spiritual and strongly believed in a God. Sharon believed in a higher power of some kind but didn't think it was God in the traditional sense. Daniel, on the other hand, hand not believed in God on Earth, and had not practiced any religion. He now knew there was more to life, that was obvious, but he still had a lot to wrap his mind around.

"Do you think we should try to track done the blaggard Guardian?" William asked bringing everyone out of their meditative moods.

"Does it matter?" Daniel answered William's question with his own. "Let's face some facts; tracking them down would take real honest-to-goodness police work. Not the kind of work we do now, which is more transporting violators than anything else." He equated Guardian work with that of U.S. Marshals on Earth.

He continued, "We would have to investigate leads, question suspects, and try to build a case. And to what end? There are no courts or prisons. The only punishments I've seen are either scaring the hell out of a violator or in extreme cases sending them to Hell."

"I wouldn't say that is all we do," William said with conviction. "We have some discretion and leeway. So it might not be real detective work, but it is more than just enforcement."

"I'm not trying to diminish would we do," Daniel had not intended to hurt his partner's feelings. "I just don't think our set up is conducive to tracking people down on our own. That's all I meant."

"Of course that's true, William added. "So all we can to is our job, but mark my words, if a situation arises where someone needs my help, I am helping."

"Here, here," Daniel responded as the women smiled.

Later, as time goes in Heaven, the Gales had decided to join Daniel and Sharon for a sail on Daniel's boat. In Daniels time on Earth sailing was a sport and a form of recreation so he found it intriguing that his two guests lived in a time when sailing ships ruled the seas.

"When I was a lad," William said after boarding *Old Man Time* and taking in the surrounding nautical atmosphere, "I used to go down to the Thames and which the ships come in. The magnificent clipper ships with tea and other luxuries from the Orient, the schooners from the continent and so many small sailing craft and fishing boats that I could never understand how they stayed out of each other's way. For a time I thought about joining the East India Company."

"Why didn't you?" Sharon asked.

"Those ships were gone for months and sometimes years at a time and I had to look after my mum and three sisters."

"Well it wasn't long after your time that the great sailing ships were gone," Daniel said as they motored their way out of the harbor. "The great wooden vessels of your youth were replaced by steel giants, and the sails were replaced with steam and that was replaced by internal combustion engines. Like the one that's moving this boat, though the ones on ships are about a thousand times larger. It also wasn't long until all almost all ocean passenger travel was replaced by jet airplanes." Daniel wondered if the Gale's already knew of the changes and he asked them.

"We know of the changes on Earth," Elizabeth answered. "We meet more modern people who take us to their more modern existence or tell us about the changes. It's really quite fascinating and you will soon be experiencing the same thing."

"When I found out about air travel, and not balloons I was surprised," William said. "But then when I found out they humans had been to the moon I almost thought it was a lie."

The sailing was great. William seemed to relish any job he was allowed to do on the boat and Sharon was more then happy to relinquish her role as sole crew member. She was speaking with Elizabeth when she turned to Daniel. "Daniel, when we were visiting the Gale's you mentioned that you were not very sad when your father passed on. Now I know you were not close but you must have been a little sad."

Daniel explained the relationship, or lack there of, between him and his father. Mainly for the Gales' edification since he and Sharon had spoken of it often.

"So it was your father who made you lead an unhappy life?" Sharon asked.

"Well my life wasn't really unhappy. I just didn't accomplish what I wanted."

The wind shifted and Daniel said loudly, "Prepare to come about."

William now very adept at following sailing orders loosened the jib sheet and as Daniel yelled, "Come about." He let it go of the line so the sail could slide to the other side as the boat was placed on a new tack.

"So your father kept you from accomplishing your goals," Sharon persisted after the boat was settled on its new course.

"I didn't say that Ms Jaffe,' Daniel answered in mock disgust. "And I know what you are doing."

"And what would that be, Mr. Lambert.

The Gales were amused at the back and forth and didn't say a word.

"You're trying to get me to re-evaluate my relationship with my father."

"Well it sounds like your father wasn't perfect but I don't think you were the perfect son either."

"No I wasn't," Daniel said a little sheepishly.

"And you at least had a father." Daniel knew what was coming as Sharon continued, "My parent's were taken from me when I was so young."

Daniel put his arm around her, steering the boat with his bare foot. The Gales both smiled—William at Daniel's foot action, Elizabeth at his arm action.

"Why don't you go find him," William said. "For God's sake man, you are a Guardian and should have no problem locating him. Even though you think we don't have any extra ability, trust me, we do"

Sharon looked at Daniel hopefully. "I rediscovered my parent's in Heaven and they rediscovered me. Maybe you and your father can do the same."

"The Professor felt that God, or the powers that be as he would say, decided when and how people hooked up in heaven" A pall of sadness enveloped the mood on the boat when Daniel mentioned their friend.

"Yes but that dear man kept trying and didn't stop until he succeeded," Sharon said adamantly. "At least you could try."

"Maybe you're right," Daniel said and added after a pause. "But only if you go with me."

"Of course I will my dear."

Sometimes Daniel liked the whole ritual of bringing the boat back to dock and making everything ship shape. But he also like the fact that he didn't have to and could come and go as he pleased. This was a case that demanded quick action so since his arm was already around Sharon he thought; *my childhood home*. The look on the Gale's faces was priceless as he and Sharon disappeared.

Chapter 23

Daniel and Sharon were standing in front of a typical 21st century suburban neighborhood—one that Daniel knew very well. There was Corky's house, empty he assumed since Corky, his best childhood friend, and his family were still alive, *well at least they were when he had died.* He wondered if they had gone to his funeral or if they had even known he died. All during the elemantary schools years Daniel and Corky had been inseperable. They had explored their small world together and the memory of the fun they had brought a smile to Daniel's face.

Directly in front of them Daniel stared at his childhood home. He was filled with a multiplicity of feelings. Though he did have fond memories of life there, he was also feeling some dread that he actually might see his father. The single car garage was open though he couldn't see in it because of the afternoon sun in his face. He wondered if he'd find his mountain bike there propped up against the wall waiting for a rider who never came anymore. He thought about the day he had left for good. He could hear his mother crying and emploring his father to do something.

"He's a man now and he makes his own choices." Were the

last words he heard as he started his pick up and drove away. They were also the last words he ever heard his father say.

The next time he saw his father he was in a casket. He had died suddenly from a heart attack and Daniel had come to the wake and funeral at his mother's request. He remembered staring at his father laying there—no longer the strong, larger than life presence of his youth—an empty vessel with an unatural skin color. It was then that Daniel had felt the emptiness he had described to his friends; it was then that he also felt no sadness.

He thought of his mother and hoped she was doing well. He should have spoken to her more during his life and promised himself he would when she died. *Promises in death were the same as in life*, he thought. *Easily made, easily broken.*

Sharon put her hand in his and they began walking up the short driveway. As if having an epiphany Daniel knew his father was here, he didn't know how he knew, but he knew. And there he was standing at his workbench in the garage. *Going to the garage to piddle*, his father would say when he wanted time alone.

"Still piddling" he said as he walked up behind his father.

"Danny" his father said as he dropped the tool he was holding and turned to face him.

"Hi Dad."

"Hi son," his father said and Daniel noticed tears welling up in his eyes.

* * *

In a whole other existence, in a completely different world an attractive middle-aged woman and her very beautiful young daughter were watching a stranger put a DVD in their player.

"Now who are you again?" the woman asked the man. "And why are you in my home?" She wasn't at all afraid of the man he had seemed honest enough. Though her ex-husband would have had fit if he knew she had let a stranger near their daughter.

"As I said, I'm a ghost hunter," the man said with a completely straight face. "I was doing an investigation in an old hotel out west. My assistant and I were in a room when... Well just watch." He turned on the VCR and forwarded to the spot he wanted.

They watched as a pen rose in the air, by itself, and began to write on the paper.

Please tell my daughter, Carrie, that I love her and that her daddy is fine and wants her to enjoy her life. My name is Daniel Lambert and I was a police officer in Frederick, Maryland.

Tears were running down the mother's face but the daughter smiled and said, "I love you too daddy."